CW01501789

MURDER OF A FAKE DIVA

A LADY MARGOT BLACKWELL MYSTERY

AMBER CREWES

PEN-N-A-PAD PUBLISHING

OTHER BOOKS IN THE LADY MARGOT BLACKWELL MYSTERY SERIES

Murder of a Fake Diva

Murder of a Notorious Gentleman

Murder of a Greedy Accountant

A LADY MARGOT
BLACKWELL MYSTERY

BOOK ONE

1

---

*L*ady Margot Blackwell stood at the top of Blackwell Manor's sweeping front steps, perfectly poised beneath her parasol. The spring of 1923 had been unusually warm, and today the sky hung in a dull, grey sulk, threatening drizzle but failing to produce it—a particularly annoying sort of English weather. Margot didn't mind. As the gracious, if occasionally sharp-tongued, owner of Blackwell Manor, she knew moments like this—the arrival of illustrious guests—were all about presentation. No theatrical pause could outshine her estate's ivy-cloaked facade and the satisfyingly grand crunch of the gravel drive beneath the oncoming motorcar's tyres. Her audience, Stella Wickham, her relentlessly quick-witted lady's maid, was unimpressed.

"You'd think they were bound for Westminster Abbey on coronation day," Stella remarked dryly, her arms crossed as she pitched her voice just loud enough for Margot to hear.

"Now, now," Margot replied, glancing back with a glimmer of humour, "if you can summon such pith just watching their arrival, I fear for their morale when they step out of the car."

It took some time, but the grand motorcar eventually slid to a halt under the manor's imposing shadow. Blackwell Manor stood like a fortress, its stone seemingly alive with the weight of history, and few visitors failed to feel its quiet authority. Margot's expression softened as the chauffeur emerged, uniform impeccable, and made an exaggerated show of opening the passenger door. At last, the show had begun.

The first to stumble out (and it truly was a stumble) was Jacques Maroni, Madame Celeste's manager. A man about as subtle as a music hall poster, Jacques was all pointed gestures and slicked-back hair, his enthusiasm for being noticed second only to his flair for melodrama. He rushed towards Margot with a beaming smile that appeared surgically grafted onto his face.

"Lady Blackwell!" Jacques exclaimed, arms outstretched as if about to embrace her; Margot countered with one strategically raised eyebrow. "It's a pleasure to finally bask in the splendour of Blackwell Manor."

"Mr Maroni," Margot replied, elegantly dodging his enthusiasm, "welcome. I trust the journey from London has prepared you for the quiet pace of country life."

Jacques blinked, momentarily confused, before catching on. "Ah, yes. A tranquil retreat. Just what dear Madame needs."

The 'dear Madame' in question appeared next, descending from the car with an air of practiced grandeur. Madame Celeste, the famed opera singer, and Margot's most demanding houseguest to date, had an undeniable presence. Wrapped in deep violet velvet, her hat a cascade of feathers that would have sent pigeons into revolt, she paused dramatically as if waiting for unseen applause. Yet as she lowered her gaze to Margot, her weary eyes betrayed more than the usual fatigue of travel.

"Madame Celeste," Margot greeted her warmly, taking the singer's hand. "Blackwell Manor welcomes you."

"And I take that welcome with gratitude," Celeste replied, her voice the low purr of a prima donna, smooth but with an edge that hinted at years of battles fought off the stage. "This haven will be most cherished."

Behind her, the entourage began to emerge like supporting cast members in one of Celeste's operatic productions. First came Irene Castell, her assistant, a young woman of unrelenting nervous energy, who stumbled over her own feet but managed to clutch a stack of hatboxes with surprising dexterity. If loyalty were an Olympic sport, Irene would undoubtedly win gold, but there was desperation in her smile that Margot found unnerving.

Next, Augustus Lambrook, the composer, emerged with a more subdued demeanour. His unkempt air and brooding countenance made him look like a man who composed at ungodly hours by candlelight. He offered Margot a stiff nod, his discomfort in the countryside apparent.

Then, with an air of calculated precision, Evelyn Linwood appeared. The vocal coach, imposing in her tailored coat and severe hat, had a face as sharp as her words were rumoured to be. Evelyn surveyed the scene as though mentally correcting it for amateurish blocking. She offered Margot a perfunctory nod and swept past her, already barking instructions at Irene about luggage.

Margot watched them all with curiosity masked as polite interest. The tension in the group was almost palpable; the kind of tension born not of weariness but of grievances left to fester too long. Even a lesser detective than Margot could see these were not companions at ease with one another but characters locked in an unspoken play of alliances and rivalries.

Madame Celeste's visit to Blackwell Manor had been arranged several months prior, when Margot's distant cousin —an enthusiastic patron of the arts—had suggested the famous soprano might benefit from the tranquillity of the countryside while recovering her voice. The manor's reputation for discretion made it an ideal retreat for someone of Celeste's stature seeking respite from the constant scrutiny of London society. What had begun as a simple favour to family connections had now evolved into something far more complicated, with Celeste's entire entourage descending upon Blackwell like actors taking their positions on a stage. Margot had expected to host a recuperating diva, not a troupe carrying enough secrets and tensions to rival the most dramatic of operas.

"Luggage to follow, madame?" Stella asked quietly once the entourage had disappeared inside.

Margot tilted her head, listening for the faint strains of Jacques attempting to charm Mary, their jittery maid. "Have someone stand guard over the china while they're here, Stella."

The maid cracked a rare smile, though her gaze followed Madame Celeste's faltering step with a trace of scepticism. "She doesn't half look the part, does she?"

Margot followed her gaze, observing how the singer's hand trembled as she grasped the banister. "No," she replied thoughtfully. "I wonder how much of that is exhaustion from the journey. Or perhaps... something else."

———

Inside, introductions began in earnest. The staff, led technically by Margot but shepherded unofficially by the formidable Mrs Henshaw, filed into the drawing room as the entourage settled. Margot hosted with the skill of her station, her tone that perfect blend of warmth and command that placated both houseguests and housemaids alike.

"Jacques Maroni, ever the tireless manager," Margot said with a silken edge, gesturing to Jacques, who beamed like a stage actor at curtain call. "And Miss Irene Castell, assistant to Madame Celeste and, I daresay, the fearless guardian of her hatboxes. Some whisper she's an undiscovered musical prodigy. Europe's opera houses had best brace themselves."

Mary, the ever-clumsy maid, blushed bright pink and curtsied so deeply Margot feared she might topple. Behind her, Stella snorted softly.

"Augustus Lambrook, our prodigious composer," she continued, watching as Augustus nodded silently at no one in particular.

"And Evelyn Linwood," Margot finished, glancing towards the vocal coach. "Vocal coach, advisor, and, I imagine, the keeper of some very select confidences."

"And discipline," Evelyn added briskly, her cold gaze sweeping over Mary and the fidgety Tom. "It's something I expect from everyone."

Mrs Henshaw's lips tightened, only slightly, as she stepped forward. "I'll see that the guests are comfortable," she said firmly, making no effort to hide her dislike of Evelyn's tone.

Tom, meanwhile, was transfixed by Celeste, and Stella muttered, "If that boy starts serenading her, I'll sew his lips shut."

As the entourage dispersed to their quarters, Stella leaned in quietly. "The only thing holding that lot together is Celeste's wardrobe."

"Nonsense," Margot replied with mocking brightness. "What holds them together is their shared suspicion of one another. Far more reliable."

But as Celeste reached the top of the stairs, turning back as though she might speak, Margot caught a glimpse not of suspicion or theatrical posturing. For the briefest moment, the diva seemed unguarded and uncertain—a woman teetering on a silent precipice.

"Far more reliable," Margot repeated, though now it felt like a question more than an answer.

2

The dining room of Blackwell Manor glittered—polished silverware, candlelight from the grand chandelier casting playful shadows across the mahogany. Margot, eagle-eyed and ever the consummate hostess, sat at the head of the table, smiling as wine glasses clinked and polite laughter filled the space. It was a scene of genteel civility, or so it seemed on the surface.

Madame Celeste, seated closest to Margot, was resplendent in emerald silk, though her perpetually furrowed brow betrayed an unease that contrasted starkly with her glittering jewels. Across from her sat Evelyn Linwood, the vocal coach whose hawkish gaze lingered over the soup course as if critiquing its performance.

"I do hope," Evelyn began in clipped tones that carried over the quiet murmur of conversation, "that these little detours from your practice schedule won't further impede your... vocal recovery."

The table stilled.

"Evelyn," Jacques Maroni, balanced between irritation and condescension, set his wine glass down a shade too firmly. "This is hardly the place to discuss Celeste's artistic matters."

Celeste's thin fingers trembled slightly as she reached for her glass, though she smiled with the practised grace of someone too used to staving off discomfort in public. "It's merely a dinner," she murmured. "We're not dissecting Wagnerian operas here, Evelyn."

"But perhaps we should be," Evelyn persisted, leaning forward in a way that reminded Margot of a sparrow pecking at freshly sown seeds. "Your recent performances have lacked coherence... fire... or even sufficient projection, and if you're unwilling to take feedback—"

"And if you're unwilling to keep your critique to a rehearsal, Evelyn," Jacques interrupted with a gleaming smile that didn't touch his eyes, "then you're the one jeopardising her recovery."

Margot had never met a dinner table that didn't relish a little tension, especially when she had no stake in the powder keg erupting before her, but even she began to sense the discomfort of her other guests. Augustus Lambrook shifted uncomfortably in his chair, retreating deeper into the protective cocoon of his own thoughts. Irene Castell, by contrast, leaned so far forward in her chair she looked on the brink of proposing sainthood for Celeste.

"Madame Celeste is perfect," Irene exclaimed with such fervour it bordered on tragic. "Perfection needs no fireworks of projection! I'd rather hear her whisper than endure ten of those so-called 'stage sopranos'."

The contradiction with Evelyn's sharp assessments was impossible to miss. Margot regarded them all with the air of a chess player observing very nervous pawns, wondering who might throw the first metaphorical punch. Evelyn muttered something unintelligible under her breath and returned to dissecting her pheasant, while Jacques began what Margot could only describe as a strained lecture on the financial risks of unnecessary criticism. For a moment, she glimpsed something beneath his theatrical facade—a flash of genuine fear. He wasn't merely posturing; he was desperately trying to maintain control of a situation spiralling beyond his grasp. His theatrical nature wasn't just vanity, she realised, but armour against a world that had taught him vulnerability was weakness. Augustus remained statuesque, staring into his wine as though the vintage might whisper epiphanies into his ear.

Quietly, Margot caught Stella's eye across the room—a lady's maid by title but an ally by temperament. Stella offered the faintest roll of her eyes as she cleared plates, murmuring just loud enough for Margot to hear, "If tensions could be bottled, your ladyship, we could skip the port and serve fury."

Margot bit back a laugh, her composure slipping for only a moment. Madame Celeste's entourage was already proving to be far more entertaining than anticipated, though she began to suspect that her own involvement might be required before long, if only to prevent combustions that would ruin the upholstery.

———

Later that evening, as the clock struck eleven, the manor had grown quiet. Guests had retired, or retreated, to their rooms, leaving Margot to relax with a novel in her hands and the comforting smell of evening jasmine wafting in from the nearby garden. *'Relax'* might not have been entirely accurate; Margot had no sooner lost herself in one particularly engaging paragraph than raised voices drifted down the corridor.

Gently laying her book aside, Margot rose without hesitation, stepping lightly as she followed the muffled argument. It led her, somewhat predictably, to Jacques Maroni's room, where another voice, sharper and punctuated with clipped syllables, gave way to Evelyn Linwood.

"I don't care what the books say," Evelyn was saying. "We agreed the budget would prioritise recovery, not appearances!"

"And appearances are everything when your income relies on illusion!" Jacques hissed back, his words like venom under the door. "She's a star! A retreat doesn't generate headlines unless there's a *performance* to justify—"

"And you think bleeding her finances dry will salvage her reputation?" Evelyn's biting tone gave way briefly to laughter bereft of humour. "You can't wring miracles out of a burned-out voice. Admit it, Jacques, you're running her into the ground, and for what? A bigger cut?"

Margot, thoroughly intrigued, shuffled backwards before her shadow betrayed her. Stella was waiting at the corner of the hallway when she returned, arms crossed and grinning.

"Funny thing about this manor," Stella remarked. "Walls thin as paper. You think the builders had an ear for drama, milady?"

Margot shook her head, though her lips pressed together

tightly to conceal amusement. "I'll remember to thank them when the tongue-lashings don't fall short of spectacular."

———

Night wore into the small hours, and just as Margot was drifting off to sleep, movement along the garden paths caught her attention. She propped herself up in bed and peered out between the curtains, squinting at the figure pacing through the hedges.

A moment later, the distinctive form of Augustus Lambrook appeared, enveloped in his overcoat and faintly illuminated by the moonlight. He moved slowly, his hands behind his back, the moonlight outlining the furrows of a man deep in restless thought.

Curiosity getting the better of her, Margot slipped on her robe and went downstairs. Cool night air brushed her face as she stepped through the French doors, surveying the composer from a distance before speaking.

"Restless nights are often best spent indoors," she called softly.

Augustus turned, startled but recovering with remarkable speed. He looked at her as though undecided on whether to explain or retreat.

"I needed air," he said simply, but there was an edge to his voice, a distance that suggested it wasn't the entire truth.

Margot took a few steps closer, her expression gentle but her mind already racing. "Air, yes. No commodity more valuable when one's thoughts refuse to settle."

Augustus hesitated, but before she could press further, he turned abruptly and moved back toward the house. "Good night, Lady Blackwell," he said over his shoulder, his tone making it clear no further conversation about his midnight wanderings would be entertained.

Margot watched him go, her brow furrowing. Whatever troubled Augustus, and Margot was certain something did, was hidden beneath more than just moonlight. As she turned back toward the path, a quiet sense of foreboding settled over her. Blackwell Manor held its secrets well, but it appeared its guests had even more to keep buried.

3

*T*he west garden of Blackwell Manor, with its moonlit arbours veiled in climbing roses and ivy, was usually a sanctuary of peace. Tonight, it was alive with tension. Margot, wrapped in a silk shawl against the cool spring air, paused beneath the twisting canopy of a rose trellis. Faint voices drifted toward her, sharp and heated, carried on the faint breeze.

Margot tilted her head, curiosity piqued. The lowered timbre of a man's voice was barely audible, the words indistinct. What did carry clearly, however, was a sharp, unmistakable phrase from Evelyn Linwood: "…stealing glory and making a mockery of promises!"

Margot stiffened, the argument slicing through the tranquil night like a reed flute's sour note. She could just make out Evelyn's outline through the thick rose bushes, her body rigid, gestures sharp with indignation. The identity of her adversary was obscured, blocked by the very plants Margot loved for their wild elegance. While the moonlight illuminated Evelyn's cutting presence, the taller shadow leaning toward her remained hidden in darkness.

"You'll regret this. Mark my words!" Evelyn's voice rose, her words ringing out in the stillness. Then came a retort, measured in tone, barely above a growl.

The argument ended abruptly. There was a final rustling movement, branches brushing against fabric, followed by the sound of hurried footsteps retreating deeper into the garden's embrace. Margot, rooted to the spot, felt her heart beat quicker. It was rare for guests at Blackwell Manor to quarrel so openly, particularly under its ever-watchful matron's proverbial nose. Yet whatever had transpired between Evelyn and the unknown figure, she doubted it rested on trivialities.

Margot hesitated only briefly. She could have called out, made her presence known. But then she remembered what Stella often said: "You learn more as a shadow than a trumpet." Curious, but not eager to embarrass Evelyn, nor lose the façade of ignorance she cherished, Margot drifted back toward the manor house. The west garden would reveal its secrets in time. Of that, she had no doubt.

———

The morning came dressed in golden sunlight, despite the weight of intrigue hanging over Blackwell Manor. Margot had just settled into a wicker chair on the terrace, scanning the day's post, when the distinctive jangle of bicycle wheels crunching over the wide gravel drive reached her ears.

Billy, the village delivery boy, charged toward them with all the exuberance of youth, his ruffled cap nearly toppling as he dismounted the creaking contraption. "Morning, Lady

Blackwell!" he called cheerfully, tipping his head in something resembling a bow.

"Good morning, Billy," Margot replied, smiling despite herself. His youthful energy was disarming, as was his chatter, which often proved surprisingly informative. "I trust Crayford's gossip tends to ride alongside you?"

Billy's freckled face split into a grin. "Oh, there's always plenty about, milady. Especially now you've got that lot under your roof." He gestured innocently toward the house, foolishly unaware of how he'd just narrowed Margot's focus.

"Do I, indeed?" she inquired, folding her hands over the sealed envelopes on her lap. "Any particular reason for such fascination?"

Billy leaned conspiratorially closer. "Well, last night, as I was headin' home through the high road—no one about but stars overhead—I saw someone by your gardens. They were moving funny-like, pacing the way my mum does when she waits for my dad to come back from the pub." He grinned cheekily, clearly proud of his metaphor.

Margot kept her tone light. "And did you see who it might be?"

Billy shook his head, his grin faltering. "Nah, the moon wasn't much help. Couldn't say if it were a lady or a gent, but they seemed... fidgety." He straightened as Stella, who'd appeared with uncanny timing, stepped onto the terrace and took the basket from Billy's arm.

"Weren't thinking to settle in for the morning, were you?" she teased, deftly shooing him off the step.

"Just bein' helpful," Billy retorted, somewhat dejected. "Good day to you, Lady Blackwell!" He tipped his cap again, then pedalled off down the driveway, his whistle sharp and carefree.

As the bicycle boy pedalled away, Margot's thoughts turned to how Blackwell Manor stood as an island of tradition in rapidly changing times. Beyond her gates, the world was embracing the dizzying freedoms of the Jazz Age—women bobbing their hair and raising their hemlines, veterans trying to forget the horrors of the Great War through dance and drink. Yet here, the rituals of country life continued much as they had for generations, though even Blackwell couldn't remain untouched by modernity forever.

Stella dropped herself into the empty seat beside Margot, shaking her head. "A charming scamp if ever there was one."

"He claims to have seen someone wandering the west garden last night," Margot noted absently, still watching the boy's retreating figure. "Fidgety," he said.

"Fidgety!" Stella smirked. "And in the west garden? That narrows down our cast of characters to… all of them."

Margot shot her maid a pointed look. "Useful observations notwithstanding, there's something more here than whimsical pacing." She paused, glancing down at the faint fold marks on the letter her fingers idly turned over. "And I suspect we're already behind on the goings-on."

"All the more reason to pay no attention to fidgeters," Stella replied lightly. "Minds unoccupied soon find themselves unravelled. Best keep yours sharp, milady."

But Margot frowned. Evelyn's voice, sharp and accusing from the night before, echoed faintly in her mind like an unresolved musical cadence.

———

By midday, the staff of Blackwell Manor was bustling about their usual business, though beneath their dutiful movements, Margot could detect a current of unease. Mrs Henshaw, the matronly housekeeper whose unshakeable poise rivalled even Margot's, approached her in the gallery shortly after luncheon. Her firm knock on the open sitting room door was enough to break Margot's reverie.

"Lady Blackwell," Mrs Henshaw began, her voice as steady as the pendulum of the manor's clock. "Might I have a word?"

"Of course." Margot gestured for her to sit, though Mrs Henshaw remained standing, her posture a reminder of her constant vigilance.

"I felt it prudent, ma'am, to mention certain… dynamics amongst your guests," she began carefully. "It seems heated words have not been confined to the recital hall."

Margot tipped her head slightly. "Dynamics or dysfunctions, Mrs Henshaw?"

Mrs Henshaw's lips twitched—an unusual show of humour. "The latter, perhaps. Miss Linwood, in particular, seems to have found herself locked in frequent disagreement with the rest of Madame Celeste's company."

"No surprises there," Margot remarked. "Evelyn does not strike me as someone one invites for her placidity."

"Indeed," said Mrs Henshaw with a hint of grimness. "Though it bears mentioning that Miss Linwood's reputation for stirring discontent is longstanding. She's a… demanding personality—difficult to ignore and harder still to placate. More often than not, she leaves ruin or resentment behind."

Margot leaned back in her chair, the edges of her mouth twitching upward in thoughtful amusement. "Sour notes, I see."

"Exactly, milady," the housekeeper confirmed. "Perhaps it's worth being cautiously aware of how such discord might play out."

Cautiously aware. The phrase lingered in Margot's mind long after Mrs Henshaw had departed, her words as meticulously chosen as the place settings they debated for every dinner party.

The garden, Billy's pacing figure, and now Evelyn's reputation for fractious relationships all pointed toward a truth buried somewhere within tangled motivations—and yet, Margot sensed this melodrama had only begun its overture.

As she gazed out toward the sun-drenched roses of the west garden, where lingering accusations and actions had cast their shadows the night before, she resolved to uncover the harmony, or cacophony, lurking beneath. After all, no mystery had ever truly thrived in the glow of Blackwell Manor's relentless hostess.

4

*M*argot knew all too well that simplicity was rarely found within Blackwell Manor's walls, despite the gentle English morning unfolding beyond them. She stepped into the drawing room, where Madame Celeste, still resplendent even in her sorrows, sat slump-shouldered in a high-backed chair. Margot hardly recognised the woman before her; this was not the radiant diva whose name adorned every major theatre in Europe. Instead, Celeste's hands trembled around the teacup she held, her once-glorious curls hidden beneath a simple scarf.

"You wished to speak privately, Madame Celeste?" Margot began with the deliberation of someone accustomed to navigating tight social mazes.

The diva did not immediately reply, her long, elegant fingers toying absentmindedly with the delicate china teacup in her lap. "Lady Blackwell," she said finally, her voice low and hesitant, "I must ask something of you... as one woman to another."

Margot arched an eyebrow, intrigued but careful. "You have my attention."

Celeste's striking features, though marred with the shadows of sleeplessness, still held traces of the beauty and magnetism for which she was revered. However, when she spoke again, that formidable veneer seemed to crack. "I have lost my voice."

Margot felt her sharp instincts rise. "Lost it? Permanently?"

A weak, trembling nod. "They cannot say, those so-called physicians. They prescribe rest, teas, tinctures. But it has been weeks—months, even—and my voice…" The final words were lost as tears began to trail down her powdered cheeks.

Margot set her teacup down and leaned forward, a blend of empathy and calculation sparking in her eyes. The loss of voice for a singer was a tragedy of operatic proportions. "You feel Evelyn suspects?" she ventured after a pause, watching Celeste's reaction closely.

Celeste winced at the name, her delicate composure unravelling further. "She doesn't just suspect. She knows I'm ruined." Her voice hardened. "Evelyn's cleverness has always been a weapon, and she will not hesitate to wield it if she finds it advantageous."

Margot's mind began piecing fragments of conversations and interactions together. What a fascinating irony it was: the great Evelyn Linwood, the unyielding vocal coach, threatening to expose the very star she helped to build. But why? And what leverage might Evelyn stand to gain? These questions simmered beneath the surface of Margot's thoughts as she placed a reassuring hand on Madame Celeste's arm.

"Take heart, Madame," Margot said softly. "You are under my roof, and I make it my responsibility to see no harm comes to my guests."

Celeste offered a faint approximation of a smile, but it carried no warmth. The tension pressing against Margot's thoughts lingered as they sat in mutual silence, enveloped by the faint strains of birdsong outside.

———

The tension that day was far from confined to the drawing room. Later, as Margot strolled the hallways on her usual rounds, the unmistakable sound of an argument, muted yet unmistakably charged, drew her toward the smaller parlour. She kept her steps light, her movements instinctively careful as she paused near the slightly ajar door.

"You're destroying her, Jacques!" came Irene Castell's sharp and trembling voice, her tone rich with indignation.

"I am *saving* her, Irene," Jacques Maroni's voice shot back, equal parts condescending and resolute. "Do you have any idea how many invitations I've turned down on her behalf? How many deals I've negotiated just to keep her presence relevant?"

"You're pushing her to breaking point!" Irene countered, her voice near a breaking sob. "All while pretending it's for her benefit, Jacques."

Margot moved an inch closer, catching the flickering silhouettes of the two combatants through the gap in the door. Irene, her face flushed and tear-streaked, stood like a trembling flame beside Jacques, who exuded his usual unflappable arrogance. He leaned casually against the mantel, his fingers worrying a cigar, though his words betrayed his calm demeanour.

"We're all under strain, Irene," Jacques replied coldly. "But unlike you, I am equipped to make the hard decisions."

The hard decisions. Margot frowned thoughtfully, her mind turning over these words. Jacques's ambition had always been abundantly clear, but the venom in Irene's tone hinted at far deeper fissures within the entourage's alliances. Yet Jacques's voice lowered suddenly, and Margot strained to catch his next words.

"Besides," he uttered darkly, just on the edge of hearing, "even Evelyn can be… managed."

Margot stiffened, her breath caught. What precisely was Jacques suggesting? Her knuckles whitened where they gripped the doorframe, but before she could decide whether to interrupt or retreat, the voices dropped and the argument ceased.

Slipping away silently, Margot resolved to keep a closer eye on Jacques and Irene. Their loyalties, it seemed, were as frayed as the diva's composure.

———

As candles flickered into life throughout the manor, an unsettling quiet settled over the house. Margot wandered the south wing, her thoughts preoccupied with the day's revelations. Madame Celeste's tearful confession, the seething argument between Jacques and Irene, all of it hinted at a storm brewing beneath the genteel facade of Blackwell Manor.

"Darkness does bring out secrets," Margot murmured to herself as she passed a shadowed arched window.

And it seemed she was not alone in feeling the weight of the evening. A high-pitched scream suddenly shattered the stillness, cutting through the halls like a knife. Margot froze, her heart racing for a split second before she sprang into motion toward the source of the commotion—the music room.

She was the first to arrive, save for Mary, the jittery maid who stood trembling in the doorway, her face deathly pale. "Milady!" she cried, her voice quaking. "It's... it's—"

Margot gently but firmly guided Mary aside, though nothing could have prepared her for the spectacle before her.

Slumped over the grand piano, Evelyn Linwood's lifeless form seemed almost grotesque in the serene setting. Her normally stern face was twisted in an expression of shock, her grey curls falling limp against the dark sheen of the piano. Most haunting of all was the wire, piano wire, Margot noted grimly, wrapped cruelly around her neck.

The room itself was eerily still, save for the faint rustle of the drapes as a breeze whispered through the half-open window. Margot's sharp eyes took in the scene as her pulse thudded loudly in her ears. Evelyn's hand rested on the piano's keys, as if in a final, desperate plea for harmony. Nearby, scattered sheet music fluttered slightly, their disarray mirroring the chaos that must have preceded her demise.

Footsteps stirred in the hallway as sleepy figures began making their way toward the scene—Stella arrived first, her sharp intake of breath the only acknowledgment of the grisly sight before them. "Well," she muttered under her breath, "this will put orchestra arrangements off for days."

Ever the stalwart, Margot regained her composure quickly. "Stella, secure the room. No one but the inspector enters until I say so."

"And the inspector?" Stella quipped darkly.

"I shall be sending for him," Margot replied.

Margot returned her attention to the lifeless figure draped over the piano. The great Evelyn Linwood, silenced so cruelly, had clearly taken her secrets with her. But Margot doubted they would remain buried for long. The curtain had fallen on Blackwell Manor's fragile peace and risen on what promised to be its most harrowing performance yet.

5

*T*he stillness of the evening at Blackwell Manor was shattered by Mary's sharp, panicked scream piercing through its elegant halls. The house, usually cloaked in the hush of late-night stillness, now buzzed like a hive stirred by a particularly irate beekeeper. The source of the chaos, naturally, was the grim sight that had greeted its occupants when Evelyn Linwood's lifeless body was discovered in the music room.

Margot stood in the grand foyer, a calming presence amidst the chaos, her gaze sharp and alert as the staff spilled from various corners of the house. Most congregated near the music room doorway, alternately gasping, whispering, or crossing themselves depending on their constitution. Margot cast a glance down at Mary, the trembling maid who had been the unfortunate soul to stumble upon Evelyn. Mary's complexion was still ghostly pale, her hands twisting anxiously in her apron.

"Mary," Margot said gently but firmly, "breathe. Hysteria will not help us now."

"Yes, milady," Mary stammered, though her eyes remained wide as saucers.

"You've done well to alert me," Margot continued, her tone steady. "Now, go with Stella and have a cup of tea. Preferably something strong."

Stella stepped forward and took Mary by the arm. "Come along then," she said briskly. "Lady Blackwell's orders. Tea first, melodrama later."

As they disappeared down the hall, Margot turned her attention back to the gathered staff. It seemed as though every footman, maid, and scullery worker had materialised to gawk at the crime scene. Mrs Henshaw, the housekeeper, was wrangling them with the efficiency of a drill sergeant, though even she looked rattled.

"Pull yourselves together!" Mrs Henshaw snapped, shooing a pair of footmen away from the doorway. "What do you think this is—the village fair? Show some decorum."

"It's just horrible," Tom the footman muttered, his usually cheeky demeanour subdued. "Miss Evelyn, dead like that… who'd have thought it?"

"Strangled with piano wire, no less," added Mary's younger sister, Betsy, her voice laced with equal parts horror and fascination. "Imagine dying amidst all that music."

"And all those sour notes," one of the maids quipped, earning a gasp and a swat from Mrs Henshaw.

"Enough!" Mrs Henshaw barked, her glare enough to silence the crowd. "You'll do your speculating on your own time. This is a household, not a clutter of hens." She turned to Margot. "Your orders, milady?"

Margot took a measured breath, exuding the calm authority that had seen her marshalling far more arduous disasters, though admittedly few as dire as murder. "Mrs Henshaw, see that none of the staff leave the estate; we'll need everyone accounted for when the inspector arrives."

She pivoted on her heel and addressed Tom, who was fidgeting with a dust cloth. "Tom, find the stable boy and send him with an urgent message to Inspector Simon Grant. Tell him there's been... an incident. He'll know what to do."

"Yes, milady," Tom said, his tone unusually sharp as he hurried off.

Meanwhile, the remaining staff, though largely obedient to Mrs Henshaw's instructions, continued to murmur amongst themselves. Margot picked up snippets of their half-baked theories as she lingered near the music room.

"Maybe it was one of the men in her party," a maid whispered to another, her tone conspiratorial. "You know how they can be; hot tempers, jealousy, and all that."

"Bah, it would have been one of 'em women," countered a footman. "There's always more spite between ladies under the same roof."

"Could have been one of those garden spirits from the old tales," chimed in Betsy with a shiver. "They don't like outsiders trampling through their territory."

Margot could scarcely restrain a smirk. If only resolving such matters were as simple as warding off garden spirits. But no, this would require wit, observation, and she suspected, a great deal of patience, especially once Simon Grant became involved.

———

The buzz of the murder spread far beyond the staff. Jacques Maroni, Augustus Lambrook, and Irene Castell, who had convened in the morning room upon hearing the news, soon arrived at the scene, their contrasting demeanours only adding to the room's volatile atmosphere.

Jacques, as always, exuded an unsettling calm. The faintest trace of a smirk played at the corners of his mouth, though whether it was nerves or something more sinister, Margot could not yet say.

"Tragic," he murmured, shaking his head as if discussing a scheduling mishap rather than a strangulation. "Utterly tragic. Poor Evelyn."

"Poor Evelyn?" Irene mumbled, clinging protectively to Madame Celeste's arm as if shielding the singer from accusatory glances. Her eyes, normally wide with nerves, were now narrowed in a mixture of outrage and suspicion. "She made everyone miserable with her sharp tongue. It's likely someone just had enough."

"Irene," Madame Celeste murmured faintly, her face ashen under layers of powder. "Please…"

Augustus, meanwhile, looked as if he might be ill at any moment. His normally stoic composure was shattered, his hands trembling as he pushed his spectacles higher on his nose. He kept glancing at the piano as though it might incriminate him with a single out-of-tune chord.

"It's…" he began, his voice faltering. "It's unthinkable. Who would… how could—"

"There's nothing to be gained from falling to pieces, Augustus," Jacques interrupted smoothly, pouring himself a cup of tea from the sideboard as though the sight of a corpse hadn't rattled him in the slightest. "Grief and shock are understandable, but we mustn't let them cloud our judgement."

"Judgement?" Irene retorted, visibly vibrating with indignation. "Really, Jacques? Acting as if this is some minor inconvenience to be *managed* along with the accounts."

"Irene, enough," Madame Celeste said again, her voice barely above a whisper.

Margot, who had leaned nonchalantly against the doorway during their bickering, finally stepped forward. "While I admire the breadth of emotions on display," she said dryly, "perhaps we might dispense with the dramatics until after Inspector Grant has arrived."

That silenced them, at least for a moment. Jacques raised an eyebrow, Augustus wrung his hands, and Irene stared at Margot with thinly veiled hostility. As for Madame Celeste, she simply looked tired, far too tired to handle the weight of her entourage's dysfunction.

———

By the time Inspector Simon Grant arrived, the tension in the manor had reached a fever pitch. Inspector Simon Grant strode into the foyer with the confident bearing of a man who had seen far worse crimes than the chaos currently unfolding at Blackwell Manor. Though normally stationed at Scotland Yard, the detective from London had been temporarily assigned to the Kent constabulary—a reassignment that some whispered was due to his unorthodox methods rather than any official policy.

This wasn't his first visit to Blackwell; a few months prior, he had successfully unravelled the mysterious death of Edwin Thistlewood, the manor's head gardener of many years. That case had revealed Grant's remarkable attention to detail and unwavering persistence—qualities that had initially irritated but ultimately impressed Margot.

She greeted him in the foyer, her usual air of composure tinged with just the faintest glimmer of mischief. She rather enjoyed watching Simon squirm under the weight of Blackwell Manor's peculiarities.

Inspector Grant, for his part, seemed resigned. "Lady Blackwell," he said with measured politeness. "Yet another tragedy under your roof, I see."

"Oh, you make it sound as though tragedies arrive with the morning post," Margot replied breezily. "As it happens, this is a most unusual case."

"They always are with you," Simon muttered under his breath.

Margot tilted her head, her expression composed. "Inspector, I assure you—I only ever intended to bring people together, not invite trouble."

Simon gave her a long-suffering look, then straightened his coat. "Where is the scene?"

"Down the hall, in the music room."

With that, the two made their way toward the heart of the unfolding mystery, a mixture of grudging cooperation and undeniable curiosity drawing them into the darkness of the unknown.

6

*I*nspector Simon Grant stood in the grand music room of Blackwell Manor, his figure cutting an imposing silhouette against the tall, mullioned windows. The air hung heavy, not just with the lingering scent of aged wood and varnish, but with a tension that had settled like mist since Evelyn Linwood's body had been discovered there. Though the body had been removed, the presence of death still clung to the room like stale perfume. The grand piano sat silent, its lid closed like a coffin. A shattered teacup, long since catalogued and bagged, left a chalky ghost-ring on the polished floorboards.

Margot stood to one side, arms crossed, her watchful eyes never leaving Simon. Though sharp-tongued and never one to defer to others without cause, Margot knew when to relinquish control. And this—murders and motives and morbid details—this was his domain. Much as she loathed to admit it.

"Let's begin," Simon said at last, his voice smooth but unmistakably commanding. It sliced cleanly through the expectant hush like a scalpel through silk. No room for dithering. No tolerance for melodrama.

Although Margot mused as she glanced toward the suspects gathered in the adjacent drawing room, with this ensemble of eccentrics, dramatics were practically a given.

Jacques Maroni was summoned first. The famed theatre manager glided into the drawing room with flamboyant grace, every inch the seasoned performer. He lowered himself into an armchair with exaggerated elegance, one leg crossed over the other, his hands smoothing invisible wrinkles in his silk lapels. The air around him smelled of bergamot and cigar smoke, both carefully selected, no doubt, for effect.

"Poor Evelyn," Jacques began, lighting one of his slender cigars with a flourish. "Sharp as a razor, that one. But no one deserves to meet their end in so violent a fashion. Quite distasteful."

Simon gave no reaction. "Where were you," he asked evenly, "during the time of Miss Linwood's death?"

Jacques took a leisurely draw from his cigar, exhaled a perfect spiral of smoke, and gave a shrug. "Retired to my quarters, Inspector. Exhausted. You've no idea the toll Madame Celeste's wardrobe takes on a man."

Simon's brow lifted, his gaze lingering on Margot for just a heartbeat longer than necessary. "Were you so fatigued that you didn't hear anything unusual from the music room?"

"Oh, I hear everything in this house," Jacques replied with a dry smirk, "but Evelyn made a habit of storming about and arguing at all hours. I'm afraid that an outburst from her didn't strike me as unique."

Margot leaned slightly closer from her place at the wall. She noted the twitch in Jacques' jaw, a small, involuntary tic that contradicted his otherwise languid composure.

"And did you quarrel with her recently?" Simon continued.

"Quarrel?" Jacques placed a hand dramatically on his chest. "Inspector, we worked together. Of course, we quarrelled. Everyone quarrelled with Evelyn. She had the charm of a wounded badger. Envious, too. She wanted to be a diva... but she wasn't. Always glancing sideways at Madame Celeste's limelight."

"Envious?" Simon asked. "Of a diva in decline?"

Jacques's lips curved into a sly smile. "Even in decline, Inspector, a star shines brighter than a shadow. Evelyn existed in the shadows. Bitter ones."

Simon made no comment, but Margot saw him scribble a note. Jacques's polished nonchalance, she decided, was just that—polished. A little too polished, to be honest.

Augustus Lambrook entered next, a gangly figure with a mop of unkempt curls and a demeanour that suggested he'd prefer to be anywhere else, preferably buried beneath a piano rather than seated across from a homicide inspector.

He perched nervously on the edge of his chair, fingers twitching at the buttons of his waistcoat. His gaze darted from Simon to the floor and back again.

"Mr Lambrook," Simon began, voice level, "we'll keep this simple. Where were you this evening?"

"Walking," Augustus said quickly. "I… I needed air. To clear my head."

Simon tilted his head. "Did your route take you near the music room?"

"No," Augustus replied, too hastily. "No, not near there. I… I stayed on the garden path. I didn't hear anything."

"Not even a raised voice? A struggle?"

Augustus's hands clenched. "I didn't hear *anything,* Inspector. I was alone."

His voice cracked slightly, and Margot caught a strange hum escaping his lips, something lilting and minor, but unmistakably out of tune.

Simon narrowed his eyes. "Are you well, Mr Lambrook?"

Augustus blinked. "I… I'm sorry. Music calms me. It's just a habit. Evelyn, she…" He faltered, then exhaled. "This is all so ghastly. I can't believe someone would want to kill her."

Margot observed him closely. There was something about Augustus's nervous energy that made it hard to tell whether he was frightened, guilty or simply terrified of appearing either.

Irene Castell followed, escorting a pale and subdued Madame Celeste into the room. Irene clung to her mistress's arm like ivy, eyes narrowed in quiet defiance. The famed soprano looked diminished somehow. Smaller than usual, her dramatic flair tucked beneath a shawl and a layer of weary silence.

Simon stood as the ladies sat.

"Miss Castell," he began, addressing the assistant, "I understand you rarely leave Madame Celeste's side. Were you with her this evening?"

"All night," Irene said firmly. "I never left her."

Simon's gaze flicked to Celeste. "Madame?"

Celeste gave a faint nod, her voice like gauze. "Yes. Irene was with me. I was… indisposed."

Margot's sharp ears caught the hesitation in her voice. Rehearsed. Thin.

"And you noticed nothing out of the ordinary?" Simon asked.

"Nothing," Irene snapped before Celeste could respond. "It was quiet."

Simon raised an eyebrow, clearly amused. "This quiet evening seems to have left everyone rather deaf."

"I resent your implication," Irene bristled. "If you think I would harm Evelyn—"

"I think," Simon interrupted gently, "that you are protecting someone. Whether it's yourself or your mistress is yet to be determined."

Celeste let out a sigh, barely audible. "Inspector, please. Evelyn… was difficult. But even difficult and phony women deserve peace."

Simon didn't respond. Instead, he scribbled a few lines in his notebook and waved them away.

As the door closed behind them, Margot leaned in. "They're hiding something," she murmured.

Simon nodded. "Every one of them is. It's just a question of *what.*"

———

The drawing room slowly emptied, leaving only Simon and Margot in the echo of polished floors and hushed voices. The inspector sat, pen tapping against his notebook, brow furrowed in thought. Margot studied him for a moment. He looked tired but focused, like a hunter who'd caught the scent but not yet the prey.

"You do have a knack for maintaining your composure," she said lightly, "even in the face of such an operatic cast."

Simon allowed himself a rare chuckle. "They'd give the Old Vic a run for its money."

Margot opened her mouth to reply but was interrupted by Stella, who appeared at the doorway with her typical unflappable air. Her expression was unreadable, but the tilt of her head suggested urgency.

"Begging your pardon, sir," she said crisply, "but I thought you should know Miss Linwood's effects have been reviewed. There's no sign of her diary."

Simon and Margot exchanged glances. The missing diary—just one more piece of the puzzle that seemed determined to remain elusive.

Simon straightened. "She kept one?"

"Religiously," Stella replied. "Pages of the stuff. Scribbling between rehearsals. Scribbling during dinner. Scribbling when she thought no one noticed. Said it helped her keep track of Celeste's requirements, though I suspect it held more venom than reminders."

Margot's brows lifted. "A diary gone missing after its owner's sudden demise? That sounds rather like motive or at least a method."

Simon closed his notebook with a snap. "Who would benefit most from it not being found?"

"Oh, anyone with secrets," Margot said. "Which, in this house, is just about everyone."

Simon nodded slowly, his eyes narrowing. "Then we must ask: what secrets was Evelyn planning to share... and who had the most to lose if she did?"

He turned toward the window, gaze dark as the storm clouds brewing beyond the manor's grounds. Somewhere in this house of whispers, lies, and performances, a killer waited. Perhaps watching them now, perhaps spinning the next deception.

Margot folded her arms and exhaled. She exchanged a knowing glance with Stella. A diary belonging to Evelyn Linwood, a woman with a penchant for sour commentary and rumoured secrets, could only mean trouble. Where had it gone?

7

_I_ t was a morning drenched in austere sunlight, the kind that made every dust mote look like drifting evidence. Margot had barely slept, her thoughts consumed by the missing diary. What secrets had Evelyn recorded in those pages, and who had been desperate enough to ensure they remained hidden? Battling both restlessness and curiosity, she found herself wandering into the west parlour, a room usually favoured by guests seeking a quiet corner for reading or clandestine gossip. The air smelt faintly of lavender polish and burnt paper.

She paused. That odour, definitely not a part of Mrs Henshaw's usual repertoire, drew Margot to the fireplace, where cold ash rested in the grate. Kneeling, she poked carefully with the fire iron, revealing a cluster of charred fragments amongst the remnants of last night's embers. Most were too far gone to decipher, but a few blackened scraps resisted the fire's appetite.

Margot retrieved a pair of sugar tongs from a nearby tea tray, such was the improvisational resourcefulness of a country matron, and fished a larger fragment free. She squinted, discerning the ghost of ink: "...too much...threat... for the sake of..." Even less legible was another scrap, the word "Evelyn" partly visible, horribly scorched.

Her heart thudded. Had Evelyn tried to destroy evidence before her death? Or had someone else, perhaps seeking to erase a dangerous secret? Margot wrapped the scraps in a linen serviette and tucked them into her pocket. She would need Stella's razor tongue, and perhaps Simon's infuriatingly logical brain, before presuming too much. All the same, her mind whirred with hypotheses as she left the chilly room behind.

———

After luncheon, the mood in the manor remained tight, with everyone going about their duties under the lengthening shadow of the investigation. Margot took solace in the gardens, the riot of primroses and irises doing little to dispel her unease. As she bent to inspect a struggling peony, she heard the telltale crunch of boots on gravel—a sound far too purposeful for a houseguest.

It was Mr Pritchard, the new gardener, waving a crumpled piece of paper in the air as if wielding a proclamation. Burly and ruddy, with soulful eyes, Pritchard never complicated anything that could be solved with compost—so his approach now, nervous and hesitant, was all the more remarkable.

"Beggin' your pardon, Lady Blackwell," he said, doffing his cap, "but I found this under the laurel by the west garden. Looks like it's been opened. Thought it might be important, what with all that's happened."

Margot took the letter from him. It felt oddly heavy, as if saturated with hidden intent. She opened it with gloved hands, scanning the erratic scrawl:

"—cannot wait much longer. You owe more than you think. If you value your reputation—or your safety—see that it's settled. No signature."

There was a small splotch of mud on the bottom edge and the faint whiff of cologne, Evelyn's notorious scent, she was almost certain, though surely that could be coincidence. Margot looked back at Pritchard. "Was it far from the path?"

He shook his head, earnest as ever. "No, milady, just behind the hydrangeas, barely hidden."

"Thank you," Margot replied warmly. "Best keep this between us for now."

As Pritchard nodded and wandered off, Margot stared down at the cryptic note, her mind spinning. Evelyn's world, already thick with threats and secrets, had grown darker with every fresh clue.

———

Inside, Inspector Simon Grant had set up a small *interrogation station* in the morning room: a circle of stately armchairs, commandeered by a man with a notebook and a steely glare. Margot found the sight faintly amusing, as if the family silver ought to tremble under his scrutiny. Simon, looking crisp and irritable in a houndstooth jacket and one of the more eccentric hats from his peculiar collection, gestured for Jacques Maroni to take a seat.

She stood by the window, half concealed behind the heavy

curtains, far enough to give the appearance of detachment, close enough not to miss a word.

Jacques planted himself with the self-assurance of a man born to velvet seats and smoky rooms. His eyes, bright and cold as bottled gin, met Simon's with relish.

"Now, Monsieur Maroni," began Simon, all brisk professionalism, "regarding the allegations of financial impropriety between yourself and Miss Linwood, there was a very heated exchange overheard the night before her death, was there not?"

A flicker of irritation passed over Jacques's face, soon replaced by his gallant manager's mask. "Heated debates are the daily bread of the arts, Inspector. Miss Linwood was... passionate, as you have no doubt heard. She was forever waving numbers and contracts at me, muttering about her own value to Madame Celeste."

"So you admit to frequent disagreements over money?"

"We disagreed, yes. But Evelyn's accusations were always exaggerated. Her ambitions far outstripped her worth. She threatened scandal, but there was nothing to it. No foundation, just the barbed words of a woman desperate to cling to relevance."

Simon did not so much as blink. "If that's the case, then you have no qualms about sharing the company accounts and your arrangement with Madame Celeste."

For the first time, Jacques looked away, fixing his gaze on a smudge of dust on the sideboard. "Unfortunately, the accounts are... presently incomplete. Evelyn believed I owed her more than was agreed. An unending cause of contention and—"

"You understand that refusing transparency does nothing to clear suspicion," Simon interrupted, his tone dry as old toast.

Jacques shot him a glance that was both withering and performative. "You may posture all you like, Inspector, but you'll find nothing to damn me. As for Evelyn, she made her bed—sadly, she did not lie in it long."

Margot could feel the tension crackling, and so, it seemed, could Simon.

"And yet she was found murdered," Simon said, "after loudly claiming someone, presumably you, had misappropriated funds. What did you do after your last argument with her?"

"I retired to my rooms, as did many," Jacques replied. "I do not make a habit of prowling the halls at midnight, if that's what you're implying."

Simon swirled his pen between his fingers, unimpressed. "And yet Evelyn wrote that someone 'owed her'—and the note found outside was unsigned. If it wasn't addressed to you, Monsieur Maroni, who could have written it? Who else had reason to fear exposure or owed her, financially or otherwise?"

Jacques gave that dangerous smile of his, all teeth. "Is everyone's dirty laundry to be aired before dinner, Inspector? Composer, assistant, diva—Evelyn was an opportunist, and she snared us all at some point."

Simon closed his notebook. "Thank you, Monsieur Maroni. Please remain available."

Jacques rose and swept out, the scent of expensive cologne and tension trailing behind him.

———

Margot lingered, catching Simon's eye once the room was empty. "You handle him marvellously well," she remarked. "He's the type to cast nets in every conversation and see what he can haul up."

Simon gave a rare, tight-lipped smile. "The trouble with men like Jacques is they're never as clever as they think, but just clever enough to cause havoc. Tell me more about the letter Pritchard found outside."

"Of course," Margot replied, retrieving the missive from her small purse. "Unsigned, but the tone is all Evelyn—woe, threat, demand, more threat."

Simon's brow furrowed as he read. "This is leverage. But where there's one note, there's often another. Perhaps even in Evelyn's lost diary."

Margot nodded, tapping her finger lightly against her skirt. "And what of the fire in the west parlour? Someone burned something important not long before the murder. All too convenient, don't you think?"

Simon considered her with that keen detective's look; part irritation, part admiration. "Lady Blackwell, if you're inviting me to break out my magnifying glass and monocle, you'll be disappointed. But—" He paused, lifting a burnt scrap Margot handed over. "—I admit, this business has room for more than one sleuth."

Stella suddenly appeared in the archway, hands on hips, and regarded them both with a faint, knowing smirk. "If you two are done planning your next opera, there's a houseful of people speculating and getting the story entirely wrong. And if anyone finds a diary, I dare say Simon's hat collection might finally meet its match."

Margot laughed, relief and camaraderie filtering into the heavy air. "Come, Inspector. Let's see who else must be prodded. The roses may be blooming, but secrets at Blackwell seem to thrive in the shade."

Simon rolled his eyes with good humour and gestured for Margot to accompany him. Two investigators, perfectly mismatched and perfectly suited for mayhem, stalking once more into the heart of the manor's intrigue.

Outside, dusk painted the gardens in fractured gold, and Margot watched the roses sway in the breeze, their thorns sharp and lovely. Evelyn's world of blackmail, debts, and betrayals was unravelling, scrap by scrap, in her hands. More clues would come, she was sure. But tonight, Blackwell Manor contained only questions and every answer was lined with ash.

8

*B*lackwell Manor was thrumming with unease, the sort that presaged a thunderstorm or, Margot reflected, a family dinner with far too many secrets on the menu. She had risen early after a fitful sleep spent puzzling over fragments of evidence burned into her thoughts as surely as they had been reduced to ash in the west parlour. If there was one truth Margot had learned as the owner of Blackwell Manor, it was that the devil was always in the details, especially where Jacques Maroni was concerned.

Margot's first errand of the day was instigated not by her head but by her hands: in the previous evening's chaos, she'd noticed a whiff of burnt paper clinging to Jacques' parlour office. Now, with the household quietly on edge and Simon Grant methodically questioning each member of Celeste's entourage and her household, Margot slipped into Jacques' study. The room was a study in controlled chaos—ledgers and concert bills arrayed in precise disarray, yet something always felt curated, calculated.

She checked the small bureau by the writing desk—locked, naturally. Margot, never without a useful hairpin (and a reputation for the mildest bit of mischief), made swift work of the lock. Inside was a stack of crisp invoices, the oldest trick in the fraudulent manager's book. Several were marked 'Celeste' in Jacque's brash, looping hand. Margot's eyes widened as she perused the evidence: not only were many sums wildly inflated, but one was a duplicate, its recipient apparently paid twice in just as many months. Margot's heart quickened as she rifled further, finding the emblems of multiple London printers on otherwise identical receipts. Forged. There could be no doubt.

She tucked the damning documents into the folds of her skirt just as a floorboard creaked in the corridor. It was Stella, pale and wide-eyed.

"Any treasure?" Stella mouthed.

Margot pressed the heel of her hand over her lips and nodded, lips twitching with satisfaction. "Sufficient gold for Simon's gallows, I dare say."

Stella grinned, then, with feline grace, she slinked away before anyone else might have reason to suspect their sleuthing.

———

The morning passed with Inspector Grant dealing out suspicion like a croupier in a casino, but Margot knew all eyes would soon turn to Jacques and his finances. She did not have to wait long. Word soon reached her that Simon wished to see her in the morning room, with Jacques and the evidence, as soon as possible.

When Margot entered, Simon looked up from a neat arrangement of files. Jacques, noticeably less at ease than usual, was seated across from him, tapping ash from a gold-tipped cigar with the deliberate care of a magician distracting his audience before a sleight of hand.

"Lady Blackwell," Simon said gravely. "You've been much occupied this morning."

"I confess, a little too much so," Margot replied lightly, laying the forged invoices on the table with a theatrical flourish worthy of the West End. "If you don't mind, Inspector, I found these whilst searching for a lost brooch. You may find them...illuminating."

Simon's eyes glimmered with admiration he tried (and mostly failed) to hide. He sifted through the papers, his brow furrowing deeper with each sheet. "Monsieur Maroni, what have you to say for yourself?"

Jacques's lips curled in an ambiguous smile. "Every penny accounted for," he replied silkily. "If there are... inconsistencies, no doubt they can be explained by the vagaries of concert accounting. The world of opera is not for the faint of pocketbook."

Margot watched as Simon held up two identical invoices, both dated within a week, for the very same stage rental in Bath. "This," Simon deadpanned, "is either an impressive coincidence or a remarkably ham-fisted attempt at fraud."

Jacques's calm flickered. His fingers, elegant and adorned with three heavy rings, drummed the arm of his chair. "Inspector," he said with sudden sharpness, "I won't deny Evelyn was... shall we say, vexed with me. She threatened to expose what she called my 'creative accounting'—such a crude term for necessary financial artistry—if I didn't advance her a bonus. She wielded it over me like a dagger at the throat of my career."

Simon tilted his head. "So, to prevent Evelyn from making your practices public, you paid her off?"

Jacques's eyes narrowed. "She was not easy to deal with. She manipulated everyone, me included! She always needed money, always threatened some new scandal if she didn't get it."

"But that doesn't answer the question," Simon replied quietly, "of whether you would go so far as to silence her permanently if the threat became too great."

A bead of sweat traced down Jacques's temple. "I... am not a murderer, Inspector. Evelyn was... an inconvenience, yes, but one I had learned to tolerate. I have managed far greater crises than a blackmailing vocal coach."

Simon didn't look away. The silence stretched, broken only by the ticking clock on the mantel.

Margot leaned forward, fixing Jacques with a steady gaze. "Why destroy the invoices, Jacques? Why risk so much, and why now, just as Evelyn threatened to go public?"

For the first time, Jacques looked genuinely anxious. His shoulders sagged ever so slightly. "You don't understand," he said, his voice dropping. "If those details came out, I'd be ruined and not just professionally. Celeste's fortune, her reputation, everything would crumble. I couldn't bear to see her dragged down."

Simon's pen scratched across the page as he recorded every word.

Before anyone could respond further, Stella appeared in the doorway, arms folded and eyebrow raised. "If charm could win a murder trial," she said in a stage whisper to Margot, "Jacques would have a jury of gossip columnists eating out of his hand."

The effect was instant. Margot's mind whirred with possibilities, her doubts about Jacques crystallising into something close to certainty. Desperation, after all, had a distinctive scent, and it clung to Jacques as surely as his expensive cologne.

———

The tension simmered as Simon dismissed Jacques, who swept from the room in a huff, flicking an accusatory glance at Margot and Stella. Alone, Margot crossed her arms and met Simon's gaze.

"You're thinking what I'm thinking," she said.

"I'm thinking," Simon answered, "that Jacques may not have strangled Evelyn, but he certainly provided the perfect motive for someone else to think he had. Financial mismanagement, blackmail, and a stage crowded with jealous rivals—it's a wonder the rest of the company hasn't cut each other's throats for curtain calls."

Stella piped up as she straightened a cushion. "Jacques could charm a gossip columnist into silence or an inspector into suspicion. But what about Celeste? She seems far too tired to plot, but who benefits most from Jacques's cover-ups?"

Margot turned the idea over in her mind, picturing Celeste and Jacques, opera and impresario, bound together, not just by contracts but by secrets, debts, and toxic loyalty.

"Keep an eye on the whole lot," she said. "Everyone here has something to lose."

Simon gave a grim nod. "Rest assured, Lady Blackwell, I mean to."

Margot gazed out the window, the afternoon sun slanting gold over the strained estate. The gardens looked idyllic, but within Blackwell Manor, motives tangled and tempers grew short. Her heart beat quickly, not just from fear but from excitement. She tasted the nearness of the truth. Jacques might now be under fire, but the real performance, Margot knew, was far from over.

9

---

*T*he morning after the confrontation with Jacques, Blackwell Manor was gripped by a hush akin to the expectant pause before a symphony's first sweet note. Margot, accustomed to managing the estate's daily melodramas, now sensed something darker and more urgent in the air. It was not simply the aftermath of fraud and murder; it was the sense that each remaining guest was holding their breath, guarding secrets as jealously as the silver in the locked sideboard.

Margot was not in the habit of taking breakfast in the formal dining room on ordinary days. It was too echoing, too full of chairs that had once been occupied by relations whose memories demanded at least a minimal reverence. But today, she sat at the far end of the dining table, close enough to the windows to catch a whiff of orchard blossom and the distant sound of the gardeners mowing lawns, their activities a strangely comforting routine in a world grown topsy-turvy.

It was there, while the household staff bustled faintly in the background and the estate itself appeared to settle into

57

another day, that she spotted Augustus Lambrook hovering by the doorway.

He looked as though he had been up all night: collar askew, cheeks drawn, eyes bloodshot behind his round spectacles. There was a gravity about him—a sense that he had carried some private burden for years and was prepared (barely) to lay it down at her feet.

"Lady Blackwell?" he said, hesitating in the half-light of mid-morning.

Margot gestured to a chair. "You must be famished, Mr Lambrook. Or do composers subsist solely on thin air and unresolved chords?"

He managed a frail smile and sat, keeping his hands tightly wrapped around his coffee cup. He glanced up, and for a split second, Margot glimpsed not the wary, evasive Augustus she'd seen in recent days, but a scared, much younger man.

"I need to speak with you," he said, his voice trembling. "Before Simon... before the inspector finds out for himself."

Margot nodded, urging him with her silence. Sometimes the best encouragement was a steady, unblinking gaze.

Augustus took a deep breath. "You know, I never much cared for Evelyn. I respected her, certainly. She was relentless—a terror in rehearsals, a force in negotiations. But she never forgot a slight, and... she enjoyed holding things over people."

"That seems to have been her favourite pastime," Margot said drily.

He coughed lightly, fidgeting with his spoon. "A few years ago, when I was still desperate for recognition, I... I made a dreadful mistake. There was a piece, a small aria I submitted under my own name, for a minor company. I'd based it, without credit, on another work. No one noticed, not at first, but… Evelyn found out. She always did. She confronted me, threatened to expose the whole affair."

Margot raised an eyebrow. "And instead?"

"I paid her." Augustus's voice was barely more than a whisper. "At first it was a token, an apology, I suppose, disguised as gratitude. But then she came to expect it. She called it a stipend to keep her in silk and champagne. She threatened me again, wrote me letters, reminders that my past lived only so long as she permitted. It was endless."

For a moment, Margot said nothing. She looked out the window, soaking in the serenity; the bees flitting between clover, the sun dappling the lawns, utterly at odds with the tangle of petty betrayals enveloping Blackwell Manor.

Augustus took another breath, his voice steadier. "The night before she… before Evelyn was killed, I couldn't sleep. My nerves were in tatters. I walked the halls, then the garden. I saw her pacing near the west end, perhaps she thought she was alone. I called after her, but she didn't stop. I tried to catch her, to beg her to let me be, but she hurried away and vanished up the path toward the house."

Margot's gaze sharpened. "Did you follow her?"

"No. I could barely keep pace. I just stood there, feeling utterly wretched. I returned inside and went to bed." He leaned forward, pleading, his hands trembling. "I swear I never saw her again. I would not, I could not, harm her."

Margot held his eyes for a long, searching moment. Augustus was many things, introspective to a fault, melancholic, often self-pitying, but she could not picture him as a killer. Still, he had much to lose if Evelyn revealed his past indiscretion to the world. And the desperation in his confession had the ring of truth, if not the clear sound of innocence.

————

The bell for luncheon rang out, trembling Margot's reverie and drawing the manor's surviving guests from their respective sanctuaries. As always, mealtimes at Blackwell Manor took on their peculiar etiquette, but today the atmosphere was different: brittle, skittish, laced with suspicion.

Margot slipped into her seat and took up her napkin with ceremonious precision, her gaze discreetly sweeping the room. Augustus slotted in beside the silent Irene, who for once refrained from fluttering over Celeste, and Jacques was late, sweeping in with a theatrical apology about 'pressing estate matters.' It was Celeste who looked most wan, cradling a cup of chamomile tea as if the warmth were the only thing anchoring her to Earth.

As soup was served and conversation started to flow, Margot kept a keen eye on Augustus. He poked half-heartedly at his food, responded to questions with the minimum of words, and jumped at every unexpected scrape of cutlery. Twice, he hummed beneath his breath; soft, repetitive, a single bar of music returning like an unresolved doubt. Not once did he address Irene or Jacques, and he left half his meal untouched.

She caught Simon's eye across the table. The inspector was watching, too, pen and notebook at the ready, looking as much a vulture as a detective.

Stella, presiding over the bread rolls with a wry smile, leaned down as she passed Margot's shoulder. "If misery could be measured in soup stains, Mr Lambrook would be a puddle by now," she murmured, lips barely moving.

Margot allowed herself a tiny smile. "Sometimes guilt is a meal best left uneaten."

————

After luncheon, Margot strolled through the gardens, mulling over Augustus's confession. One could scarcely imagine a less likely murderer: so mournful, so deeply averse to conflict. But desperation skewed the soul in unpredictable ways. Besides, Evelyn had not just blackmailed Augustus; she had actively stoked the flames of insecurity in everyone at the Manor.

She spotted Augustus standing by the fountain, staring into the water as though searching for some elusive resolution at the bottom of its stone basin. She approached, curious to probe a little further.

"Do you believe in redemption, Lady Blackwell?" he asked suddenly, not looking up.

Margot pondered. "I believe people make mistakes more often than they admit. The difference between damnation and forgiveness is usually whether one tells the truth at the right moment."

He laughed softly, without humour. "Then I'm thoroughly damned."

"Or perhaps," Margot countered, "you're merely caught in a web of regrets." She bent to pluck a stray petal from the fountain's rim. "If you're hiding more, Mr Lambrook, now is the time."

He shook his head, turning away. "You know everything that matters."

She doubted this, but let it go.

———

That evening at dinner, the frostiness among the guests made the elaborate meal—three courses, meticulously prepared by Mrs Henshaw for the inspector's benefit—feel more like an ordeal than a feast. Jacques held court from his end of the table, waxing lyrical on the difficulties of artistic management with an eye ever fixed on Simon. Irene sat beside Celeste, whose pallor had deepened to an almost ghostly hue. Augustus, by contrast, seemed to dissolve into his chair, performing a mechanical, joyless pantomime of eating.

Margot, ever sensitive to the interplay of glances and gestures, noticed that Augustus barely spoke unless directly addressed, and when he did, his answers were even more evasive than before. Once, as the conversation veered by chance toward the nature of musical adaptation and the fine line between homage and theft, he flinched, spilling wine on the white linen cloth. Margot met Simon's eyes again and saw that her instinct was echoed in the inspector's frown.

By dessert, only Stella's quips, "If anyone's pudding disappears, I shall accuse Mr Lambrook first!" raised so much as a chuckle, and even she seemed to sense the shadow in Augustus's downcast stare.

———

Later that night, Margot sat alone in the library, a single candle flickering and her thoughts spinning like a phonograph that played only in circles. Augustus's confession had certainly explained the anxiety dogging his movements, but it had also provided motive, and a reason to fear exposure almost as much as Jacques. The question asked nightly in Blackwell Manor was no longer 'who had reason to hate Evelyn?' but 'who hated her enough to kill?'

Margot poured herself a small sherry and peered out through the rain-flecked window, feeling the first true chill of late spring. Somewhere, the solution to Evelyn's murder was hiding in plain sight, wrapped in confessions that were not quite confessions, and in secrets that would not, could not, stay buried for long.

But the strangest thing, as Stella pointed out later while bringing up Margot's slippers, was not that everyone was hiding something. It was that, amid all the frantic theatre, it was still possible, through a chink in the mask, for a truth to slip out.

And Margot, ever the patient sleuth, was watching for precisely that moment.

10

*M*argot was not the sort of woman to drift aimlessly through the echoing corridors of her ancestral home. Blackwell Manor, with its marble halls and oak-panelled chambers, held a reverence for purpose, and Margot shared that trait in abundance. Her footsteps usually echoed with resolve, not hesitation. Yet on this grey, uneasy afternoon, her strides carried the weight of something less certain, an intangible sense that something in the house remained unsettled, unfinished.

Though Inspector Grant had taken charge of the investigation into Evelyn Linwood's untimely demise, the manor itself had not returned to peace. There was a feeling in the air—a dense, muffled apprehension, as though the walls themselves waited for confession.

It was this disquiet, paired with an admittedly persistent curiosity, that drew Margot back toward the music room. The space had already become infamous, the scene of Evelyn's final performance, though no applause had followed. The grand piano still stood at the centre of the room like a monument to something broken. Where once it had been a source of harmony, it now served as a chilling reminder of the discord Evelyn had left behind.

But it was not the gleaming instrument that captured Margot's attention, it was the sight of Irene Castell, sleeves rolled to her elbows, furiously scrubbing the ivory keys with such intensity one might assume they were stained with blood rather than fingerprints.

"Irene," Margot said, her voice gentle but carrying easily in the stillness.

The young woman startled, nearly dropping the cloth. She straightened at once, cheeks flushed, a sheen of perspiration forming at her brow.

"Oh... Lady Blackwell," she stammered. "I didn't hear you come in."

Margot crossed the threshold, heels whispering against the polished floorboards. She paused a few paces from the piano, tilting her head.

"Surely you're not conducting a séance through polish," she said mildly. "That piano's seen decades of use without being buffed within an inch of its life."

Irene gave a strained laugh. "Evelyn would have haunted me if I left a single smudge," she murmured. "She... she had a thing about the keys. Couldn't abide any sign of wear."

"So I've heard," Margot replied, folding her hands before her. "But I must say, your enthusiasm borders on, what shall we call it, penitential?"

Irene hesitated, cloth frozen in her hand. "She was

particular," she said, eyes fixed on the keys. "And she hated being contradicted."

Margot studied her closely. Irene's usual jitteriness had intensified into something sharper—guilt perhaps, or fear masquerading as cleanliness. Her every movement was wound tight, and though she kept her gaze low, Margot could see the rapid fluttering of her eyelids. Something was eating at her.

The moment stretched until a new voice broke it.

"I see the piano's being given its due repentance."

Augustus Lambrook stood in the doorway, his frame slightly hunched, dark circles shadowing his eyes. If melancholy had a mascot, it would have looked precisely like him.

Irene said nothing, though her shoulders stiffened.

Margot offered him a nod. "You sound unsurprised."

"Not in the slightest," Augustus said, stepping inside. "Evelyn had a knack for leaving behind a legacy of chores. I remember once she spent an entire afternoon berating me because I had the gall to rest my hand on the lid during rehearsal. Said I'd left 'oily fingerprints'." He grimaced faintly. "As though my hands were made of axle grease."

There was something bitter beneath his light tone, and Margot noted how his gaze never quite met Irene's.

"She just wanted things to be perfect," Irene muttered.

"Perfect for whom?" Augustus asked, with unexpected sharpness. "For herself, certainly. Not for anyone else."

Before the conversation could curdle into argument, a brisk voice cut through the air.

"If we're passing out indictments to the dead, I'd rather we do so over tea."

Stella Wickham swept into the room carrying a silver tray of scones and preserved lemon. She set it down on the sideboard with a practiced flourish.

"Good heavens," she said, surveying the scene. "If that poor piano had feelings, it would have filed a grievance days ago."

Irene flushed but said nothing. Augustus gave a weak chuckle that died too quickly.

"You've been busy, Stella," Margot observed.

"Someone has to keep this place from dissolving into madness," Stella replied. "And until Inspector Grant decides which of you is the villain of the piece, I suggest we all remain cordial. The dead aren't helped by sulking."

"Nor by obsessive polishing," Augustus muttered, just loud enough to be heard.

"I'm not sulking," Irene said sharply. "I'm... just doing what needs to be done."

Margot stepped in gently. "Sometimes what needs to be done is to sit and reflect."

Irene hesitated, then dropped the cloth. Her shoulders slumped as though a weight had been temporarily set aside.

"Very well," she said. "But I still say Evelyn would have disapproved."

"Let her," Stella said briskly. "She disapproved of nearly everything."

———

Tea was served in the drawing room under the watchful gaze of Margot's ancestors, their portraits solemn and unblinking in the fading light. Outside, a gentle drizzle had begun, turning the gardens into a blur of mist and glistening hedgerows. Inside, however, the atmosphere was anything but tranquil.

Margot took her tea with two sugars, stirring slowly as she observed the room's inhabitants.

Jacques Maroni stood, as usual, by the tall window, arms crossed and gaze unreadable. Augustus had claimed his favourite armchair, though he seemed to fold inward, hunched and tired. Irene sat stiffly, teacup trembling faintly on its saucer.

Stella moved efficiently among them all, distributing biscuits and tart slices with the authority of a general at the front lines.

"I dare say we're overdue for a cheerful revelation," Stella quipped, offering Jacques a second scone.

He waved her off. "No appetite."

"None of us seem to have one," Margot said. "Appetite vanishes quickly when one dines among secrets."

There was a pause. Irene sipped. Augustus stared into his cup. Jacques finally spoke.

"Secrets?" he said, voice low. "What manor doesn't have them?"

"But this one seems to specialise in them," Margot replied smoothly. "Especially those Evelyn carried with her."

Augustus stirred, setting his cup down with a faint clink.

"She knew too much," he said.

"Of what sort?" Margot asked.

"Everything," Augustus whispered. "She… listened. Observed. And she kept it all. As if she were saving it for something."

"Insurance," Jacques said. "Or blackmail. It depends on how charitable you are."

"She had a habit of collecting confidences," Irene added quietly. "Sometimes people didn't even realise they were telling her things. She was… clever that way."

"Dangerous," Jacques corrected. "And dangerous people make enemies."

Margot tilted her head. "Do they also make murderers?"

Silence answered her.

———

Later, as twilight deepened into night, Margot wandered back to the music room. The piano gleamed under the low chandelier, now quiet, untouched. She circled it slowly, trailing her fingers along the edge of the lid.

How much of the truth had been pressed into these keys?

The shadows shifted, the room sighing as if remembering its grief.

Something tugged at Margot's thoughts.

She bent closer, peering into the small gap between the piano and the floor. Just beneath the far leg, tucked where even a cleaning cloth would miss, she spotted the corner of what appeared to be paper.

Carefully, she knelt and drew it out, a torn sheet, part of a journal page, edges frayed and smudged. There was no name, but the handwriting was unmistakably Evelyn's—neat, slanted, and biting.

Margot read:

"—Jacques thinks no one notices, but I see it. The way he looks at the ledger, the strange absences. If I told Celeste, it would ruin him. Perhaps I shall."

She inhaled sharply. Evelyn had indeed been watching and writing. If this was one fragment, how many others existed? And more importantly—who knew?

She folded the page carefully, tucking it into her pocket. The silence around her deepened, not peace, but anticipation. The music room held more than memories. It held truths yet to be uncovered.

As Margot stood, she caught her reflection in the polished piano lid—still, composed, but not fooled. Somewhere within these walls, a murderer waited. And she, Lady Margot Blackwell, intended to unearth every last secret that kept them safe.

The game was still afoot.

11

The morning sunlight filtered through the mullioned windows of Blackwell Manor, casting a lattice of gold across the library's rich oak flooring. Dust motes danced lazily in the beams of light, disturbed only by the occasional turn of a page or the creak of leather as Margot shifted in her chair. Clad in a dove-grey morning gown with pearl buttons, she sat at her walnut writing desk, a picture of composed elegance. Yet the expression she wore told a different story. One of irritation, concern, and something else, something rarer: unease.

Before her lay a single envelope. No monogram. No return address. Its seal was a plain red wax circle, hastily pressed and barely holding. The contents, however, bore far more weight than its modest casing.

Stop meddling where you don't belong. Blackwell Manor isn't safe.

The words, scrawled in jagged strokes, were written with such pressure the nib had pierced the paper in places.

Margot tapped a gloved finger against her lips, the note held delicately in her other hand. Her eyes narrowed, sweeping over each angular letter. Whoever had written it possessed both haste and fury. It was not the neat cursive of someone who composed their thoughts with care. No, this was dashed off in a moment of passionate resolve or desperation.

She turned the note over. No watermark. No markings. But there were slight smudges of ink, evidence of a hurried fold. It spoke of someone unsettled. Possibly male. Possibly someone in the manor.

Jacques Maroni came to mind.

The man had a temper that simmered just beneath his urbane exterior. Sharp-tongued, intense, and prone to bursts of emotion, he had already clashed with more than one guest since Evelyn's death. But would he go so far as to issue threats? Margot couldn't say.

"Inspector Simon Grant should see this," she murmured.

She folded the note carefully, slipping it into her pocket before rising with purpose. Her heels echoed across the wooden floor as she left the library behind.

———

The south wing study, temporarily repurposed for Inspector Grant, was cluttered with ledgers, maps, and discarded tea cups. Papers had overrun the long table near the window, and the smell of tobacco hung faintly in the air despite the open casement.

Simon, sleeves rolled to the elbow, sat hunched over a notebook. His braces strained slightly across his shoulders, and a pencil was tucked behind one ear. He looked up as Margot entered.

"Lady Blackwell," he said, with half a smile tugging at his lips. "Come to offer fresh scandal for my growing pile?"

"Something rather more pressing, I fear." Margot handed him the note.

Simon read it in silence, then again. His jaw tightened. "A threat. Blunt, unpolished, and deliberate."

"I thought it might interest you."

"Indeed." He turned the paper sideways, then held it to the light. "Ink still fresh. This was written recently, last night, or perhaps early this morning. Handwriting's a mess. Untrained but forceful. You suspect Maroni?"

"His temperament aligns, as does his... theatricality."

Simon grunted. "The man certainly doesn't lack flair. But it could be anyone. Irene, perhaps. Even Augustus. We shouldn't discount desperation."

Margot tilted her head. "Desperation can take many forms. This one chose ink and intimidation."

Simon jotted a note in his ledger. "I'll have Maroni questioned again. Firmly this time."

"Do be careful," Margot said. "The man reacts poorly to being cornered."

Simon smirked. "So do most predators."

———

The house was unusually quiet that afternoon. Margot returned to the drawing room for a moment of calm and found Stella Wickham, her trusted lady's maid, dusting near the hearth.

"Any fresh mysteries today, milady?" Stella asked, feather duster paused mid-air.

"Only the usual," Margot said dryly. "Though I suspect we are no longer being observed from a distance. Someone has grown bold."

"You'll sniff them out," Stella said confidently. "You always do."

Before Margot could reply, Tom the footman appeared at the door, awkwardly holding something in his gloved hands. "Begging your pardon, Lady Blackwell, but I found this upstairs. Thought you should see it."

Margot took the object, a single white glove, soft as cream and embroidered with a letter "A" in navy thread at the cuff.

"Where exactly did you find it, Tom?"

"Just outside Monsieur Maroni's door, milady. Odd place for a lost glove, if you ask me."

"Indeed. Thank you. That will be all."

Tom departed. Margot held the glove up to the light. It was fine leather, hardly worn. The monogram, an old-fashioned flourish, was unmistakably bespoke. Likely from a Savile Row tailor. Not Jacques's taste. But Augustus Lambrook's? Entirely possible.

———

Margot found Augustus in the garden near the sundial. He sat on a wrought-iron bench, fingers steepled together, eyes lost in the rippling surface of the ornamental fountain.

"Mr Lambrook," she said, approaching.

He turned, startled. "Lady Blackwell."

She held up the glove. "I believe this belongs to you. Or it did."

His brow furrowed. "Ah. Yes. It was part of a pair. But it isn't mine now. I gave it to Maroni. He asked for one, said his had split."

"How generous of you."

He shrugged, avoiding her gaze. "I had no reason to think anything of it. Jacques can be… fastidious."

"And now it's lying outside his room, during the week of a murder, embroidered with your initial. You see how that might be… complicated."

Augustus looked stricken. "I hadn't thought… do you believe he's involved?"

"I believe nothing yet. But I trust patterns. And this one is growing more intricate by the hour."

She left him there, alone, wringing his hands.

———

Evening fell with a slow hush, the manor cast in a palette of amber and shadow. Candles flickered in the drawing room, their flames too lively for the tension that simmered beneath them. Margot sat near the fire, her cup of tea untouched.

Stella poured herself a second helping, more for something to do than thirst.

"You look like you're trying to read firelight, milady," she said.

"I may as well," Margot replied. "The people in this house are giving up no truths. Perhaps the flames will."

Stella sank into the armchair opposite. "We've got a dead woman, a frayed diary, a glove playing hide and seek, and a warning from someone with a blunt quill and a bruised ego. You'd think one of them would slip up."

"They will," Margot murmured. "They always do."

"And until then?"

Margot's gaze drifted to the window, where a cool breeze rustled the ivy climbing along the manor's walls. Her expression softened as memories flickered behind her eyes. "There was a time when this place was simply home, a backdrop to a carefree life I thought would last forever. But when I lost my parents—too soon, too suddenly—it became more than that. Overnight, Blackwell Manor was no longer just bricks and mortar; it was my responsibility." She paused, her lips curling faintly. "I admit, at first, the weight of it was overwhelming. But now... I'm its custodian, and I wouldn't have it any other way. My duty is to protect its peace."

There was a pause, then Stella said, "You think Jacques is guilty."

Margot hesitated but remained poised. "I think he's hiding something. Whether it's guilt or shame, I can't yet say. But this glove, this note, they were meant to be found. Someone wants to stir the pot. Perhaps to distract us. Or perhaps to warn us of something worse."

The fire popped, a coal collapsing into embers.

"Blackwell Manor is a house of secrets, Stella. And secrets are rarely kept without cost."

They sat in silence; the candlelight flickering like restless thoughts across their faces.

Outside, the wind picked up, whispering through the ivy-laced stones. Somewhere in the distance, a door creaked on its hinges, and the sound echoed faintly through the great halls.

Margot straightened her spine.

The house was stirring. And with it, the truth.

She would be ready.

12

———

*T*he great hall of Blackwell Manor stood in breathless silence, broken only by the rhythmic ticking of the grandfather clock nestled between two towering suits of armour. Midnight. The witching hour had crept upon the house, casting long shadows across the marbled floor. High above, the moonlight spilled through the leaded glass windows like pale ink, painting ghostly patterns upon the crimson carpets.

Margot stood poised at the landing of the grand staircase, wrapped in a silk robe the colour of midnight itself. A single lamp lit the corridor behind her, its dim glow casting her shadow down the steps. Something had stirred her from the quiet comfort of her after-dinner reflections in the library— not a sound loud enough to alarm, but rather a subtle disturbance, the kind that prickled the instincts: a creak in the floorboards, a shuffling whisper too deliberate to be the house settling.

With the grace of a cat, Margot descended the stairs, each step deliberate, silent. She crossed the hall, guided by instinct rather than intention, until she reached the glass-panelled doors that opened onto the garden terrace. There, beyond the panes, under the watchful gaze of a full moon, the hedges of the rose garden lay half in silver, half in shadow.

And amidst that interplay of light and dark, a figure crouched beside a flowerbed.

Margot opened the door quietly, her slippers soundless against the gravel path. The air was cool and heavy with the scent of earth and lingering roses. As she approached, her voice broke the stillness.

"Augustus Lambrook. What, pray, are you doing out here at this hour?"

The composer's head snapped up. His face, usually pale, was now flushed with exertion or guilt, and his hands were coated in dirt. For a breath, he seemed frozen by her presence, a man caught mid-crime, though his crime remained unknown.

He stood, brushing soil from his fingers with little success. "Lady Blackwell," he said, attempting a smile. "I couldn't sleep. The roses... they looked hauntingly beautiful in the moonlight. I thought they might stir a melody." He gestured vaguely at the flowerbed, as if hoping it might support his flimsy excuse.

Margot crossed her arms, unconvinced. "Indeed? And do your compositions often require the accompaniment of garden spades and muddy fingernails?"

Augustus laughed weakly. "Only when inspiration proves elusive. I suppose I let curiosity get the better of me."

Her eyes moved past him to the soil he'd been disturbing.

There, half-buried, something metallic caught the moonlight. She tilted her chin toward it.

"And that? Was it part of your muse's offering?"

He followed her gaze and blanched. "It's nothing. Just... something I unearthed accidentally. Junk, I'd wager."

Margot arched an eyebrow. "I would very much like to determine that for myself."

Without waiting for permission, she stepped forward and knelt, brushing away soil. What emerged was a small, tarnished locket—not junk, certainly. The clasp was broken, the chain partially snapped, as though it had been yanked with force.

"Fascinating," she murmured.

Augustus shifted uncomfortably. "I didn't see it until you arrived, I swear it."

"Then your muse has rather peculiar taste," Margot replied. She rose, pocketing the locket. "Do see to your hands, Mr Lambrook. And perhaps find your inspiration in less suspicious places."

Without waiting for a reply, she turned and strode back toward the house, the night swallowing the sound of her departure.

———

The following morning dawned grey and listless, the manor swathed in mist. Margot, seated at her breakfast table with a slice of toast and a poached egg, was deep in thought when Stella Wickham entered, her boots still damp from the dew-laden grass.

"You'll want to see this, milady," Stella said without preamble, holding out her hand. In her palm lay a brooch, its design delicate and unmistakably feminine—a ring of tiny enamel forget-me-nots surrounding a central garnet.

Margot's eyes narrowed. "Evelyn Linwood's brooch."

"Aye," Stella said, placing it on the table. "Found it near the garden gate, tucked in behind a hedge. As if someone dropped it in haste, or meant it to stay hidden."

Margot picked it up delicately. The clasp was bent, the enamel slightly chipped. "I remember her mentioning it. A gift from her mother, if I recall. Sentimental and valuable."

"Odd place for a keepsake to end up," Stella said.

"Very odd indeed."

Not long after, Mrs Henshaw arrived in Margot's study, her usual stiff composure tinged with unease.

"Lady Blackwell, I hesitate to bring gossip, but... I saw Monsieur Maroni near the garden gate last night. Very late. He was agitated. Muttering to himself."

Margot looked up sharply. "What was he doing?"

"I couldn't say exactly, but he had something in his hand. Small. He was speaking French, low and hurried. I didn't want to disturb him."

"Did he see you?"

Mrs Henshaw shook her head. "I don't believe so."

"Thank you, Mrs Henshaw. Your discretion remains invaluable."

The housekeeper gave a firm nod and withdrew, her sturdy heels clicking softly on the floorboards.

As Mrs Henshaw departed, Margot reflected on the intricate balance of Blackwell Manor's hierarchy. The staff knew everything, yet were expected to act as though they knew nothing. They moved through rooms like ghosts, privy to the most intimate moments of their employers' lives while remaining invisible themselves. It was an arrangement as old as the manor itself, yet one that required constant, unspoken negotiation. Mrs Henshaw, with her starched apron and iron dignity, was as much a guardian of this tradition as Margot herself.

———

Seeking further clarity, Margot climbed to the sewing room, where Irene Castell was patching a frayed hem. The young woman looked up, her expression wary but polite.

"Miss Castell," Margot said, drawing the brooch from her pocket, "does this look familiar?"

Irene's breath caught. "That's Evelyn's."

"It was found in the garden. The clasp is damaged. Did you ever repair this for her?"

Irene hesitated, then nodded. "Yes, a few days ago. It had come loose. I used silver thread to reinforce the catch."

"Would anyone else have access to that thread?"

Irene glanced toward the sewing basket. "Anyone, I believe. It's freely taken whenever needed—never kept under lock and key."

"Do you recall if anyone showed unusual interest in the brooch?"

"No," Irene said quickly. Too quickly.

Margot studied her for a moment longer. "Very well. Thank you."

———

Back in her study, Margot laid out the morning's discoveries before her like cards in a solitaire game. Augustus in the garden, his fingers stained with soil; Jacques near the garden gate, muttering to ghosts only he could see; the brooch, wrenched from Evelyn's person and left abandoned in the dark; and the locket, dug up like an unspoken secret.

Each clue sang a different note. But they belonged to the same song.

As dusk began to gather, Margot stood at the window, watching fog roll across the lawn. The truth, she knew, would not come easily. Blackwell Manor was full of careful lies and half-hidden truths. But like all good music, the key would eventually resolve.

And when it did, Margot would be ready to conduct the final movement.

13

---

argot's evening began not with a dramatic thunderclap or a mysterious letter slid beneath her door, but with the soft rustle of velvet and lace— an altogether quieter intrusion, yet no less portentous. Madame Celeste arrived at the drawing room just as the clock in the hall struck half-past eight, her expression drawn in theatrical sorrow. Draped in elegant melancholy, she looked every inch the tragic heroine of a forgotten play, her eyes rimmed with fatigue and her fingers nervously fidgeting with the delicate edge of her velvet shawl.

"You look burdened, Celeste," Margot said mildly, though her eyes sharpened. She gestured to the armchair opposite her own. "Has another secret spilled into the roses?"

Celeste offered a wavering smile that barely touched her lips. She lowered herself into the chair as though the weight of the evening were pressing down upon her spine. "No fresh revelations this time," she murmured, gazing at the fire as though she might divine answers in its dancing flames. "But I—" She paused, swallowing the words she hadn't yet spoken. "I must confess, the longer Evelyn's shadow hangs over this house, the harder it becomes to breathe."

Margot tilted her head, curiosity piqued. "A shadow as heavy as one's sins often are," she remarked, watching the woman closely. "And whom, Madame, do you believe bears the most weight?"

There was a pause, a silence thick enough to be cut with a knife. Celeste's eyes flicked toward the fire again, searching for something—courage, perhaps, or forgiveness. "I regret…" she began, then faltered. "There was a time I treated Evelyn more as a business partner than a friend. A sour-faced conspirator in the theatre's politics, tangled and thorny beyond measure. But I was desperate, Margot. She had influence, and I… I was drowning."

Margot said nothing, simply allowed the woman to speak, the confession spilling like wine from a cracked goblet.

"She knew things," Celeste continued, her voice barely above a whisper. "Secrets Augustus hoped to bury. She unearthed them like a hound and used them mercilessly. She could make anyone feel small… especially those with soft hearts."

"Augustus feared her?" Margot asked, leaning forward slightly.

Celeste nodded slowly. "Yes. Terribly. More than he feared disgrace or failure. Evelyn had a way of twisting the truth into a blade. And he… he always feared being exposed."

Margot's gaze drifted to the hearth rug, where the fire cast shadows that seemed to curl and reach across the floor like fingers. Augustus Lambrook, whose nocturnal garden exploits already painted him suspicious, now emerged anew in the portrait of guilt, framed this time by fear and manipulation. Yet fear alone did not a murderer make.

She stood, restless. "Thank you for your honesty, Celeste. Whatever truths remain, they do not hide well forever, not within these walls."

Celeste gave a wan nod, and Margot left the room, her thoughts prickling.

———

As the night deepened, so too did Margot's restlessness. She paced the corridor near the library, the hush of the old manor pressing close. The wall sconces flickered in response to a draft, and for a fleeting second, she felt as though the house itself were listening.

She was rounding the corner toward the east wing when Tom, the ever-earnest footman, came scampering up the hallway, clutching an envelope as though it might combust in his hands.

"Lady Margot!" he called breathlessly. "Billy sent word just now. Says he saw someone before dawn, lurking near the music room."

Margot raised a brow. "Lurking?"

"Well, he didn't say it like that exactly," Tom admitted. "But he said the man was walking with a limp. Said it gave him a fright."

"A limp," Margot echoed, her mind already assembling the image. "And he didn't attempt to follow?"

"No, milady. He... said something about not wanting to get involved."

Margot gave a rueful smile. "Very sensible of him."

But her thoughts churned. A limp. It could point to Jacques Maroni, whose uneven gait and volatile temperament had made him both a favourite and a suspect in equal measure. Was this yet another thread of suspicion to knot around his name or simply a case of convenient coincidence?

"Thank you, Tom," she said at last. "Tell Billy I appreciate his diligence, however delayed."

Margot stood by the window, watching the garden paths. The limping figure troubled her, not just for the mystery it presented, but for what it revealed about Blackwell Manor itself. The house had become a stage for secrets, every corridor a potential hiding place, every shadow suspect.

She recalled how Augustus had moved through the garden nights ago, the way his shoulders had hunched forward as though carrying an invisible weight. Jacques, too, had a particular way of walking—a slight hesitation in his left leg from an old riding accident he'd once mentioned. And even Irene, usually so poised in Celeste's presence, sometimes favoured her right foot when she thought no one was watching.

The household was full of limps and limping, both literal and metaphorical. Everyone carried their burdens awkwardly, unevenly. And someone among them had left tracks that Billy had noticed.

"A limping figure in the darkness," Margot murmured to herself. "How perfectly theatrical."

No sooner had Tom scurried off than the long, straight-backed silhouette of Inspector Simon Grant appeared at the far end of the hall, notebook in hand and eyes narrowed in focus.

"I've questions," he announced, even before reaching her.

Margot lifted a brow. "Join the queue."

Simon's tone held little humour. "This sighting, a man with a limp, matches Jacques. And you'll admit, he's been evasive since day one."

"He's also been bullied, questioned, and watched like a hawk," Margot replied. "Fear breeds evasiveness. It does not confirm guilt."

Simon glanced down at his notes. "Even so, Jacques was seen near the garden gate. Near the brooch. He has motive, perhaps one we've not yet uncovered. Evelyn threatened him too, didn't she?"

"So we've heard," Margot said. "But hearsay and murder are poor bedfellows."

Simon frowned. "Well, here's the twist. At the exact time Billy claims to have seen the limping figure near the music room, Jacques was in the kitchen, pleading with Cook for a late-night tart."

Margot blinked. "A tart?"

"Rhubarb, apparently. Two of them confirmed it—Cook and young Mary. He was dramatic about it, something about insomnia and low blood sugar."

Margot could almost picture it: Jacques, flailing arms and flustered, bemoaning his fragile nerves while nibbling at a tart. The image didn't fit the more sinister tapestry others painted.

"So he's momentarily absolved?" she asked.

Simon gave a reluctant nod. "Temporarily. Though I never trust anyone who favours rhubarb."

Margot smiled faintly. "You should interrogate more pies."

———

The hour turned late. With each new detail, Blackwell Manor seemed to swell with unresolved tension. The chandelier above the staircase shivered with a breeze no one could locate. Doors creaked softly without reason. Somewhere, a grandfather clock chimed its lonely tune.

Margot returned to her study, where a fire still burned low in the grate. The glow cast long, wavering shadows across her desk, its surface cluttered with notes, a pocketbook, and the infamous brooch, Evelyn's brooch, gleaming softly in the firelight.

Her gaze dropped to it, fingers brushing the delicate enamel petals. So small, so seemingly insignificant. And yet it had turned the investigation in circles.

A soft knock drew her attention. Stella stepped inside, bearing a cup of tea on a tray. "Thought you'd need this," she said.

Margot accepted it with a sigh. "I'd hoped for a conclusion. Instead, I have a headache."

"Well, you've more patience than most," Stella said, settling onto the edge of the opposite chair. "Half the village would've thrown in the towel."

Margot took a sip of the tea and considered her maid's unwavering composure. "The trouble is, Stella, they all seem guilty. Every one of them. Celeste with her regrets and murky alliances. Augustus skulking in gardens with soil on his hands. Jacques with his limp and rhubarb. Irene with her trembling silences. Even Simon has too much interest in neat conclusions."

Stella leaned back, folding her arms. "Well, Evelyn didn't die by accident. So someone's truth is a lie."

That thought settled between them like a stone.

Margot reached again for the brooch. "This—this brooch—wasn't merely misplaced. It was ripped off, the clasp twisted. Whoever left it near the gate wanted it to be found, or feared it would be."

"Too deliberate for an accident, then?" Stella asked.

"Far too."

The fire crackled softly. Somewhere in the distance, the wind rustled against the ivy-draped walls. And in that dimly lit room, Margot felt the pieces shift again.

Everyone had a reason to hate Evelyn Linwood. But motives alone meant nothing unless tethered to time, to place, to something tangible.

She rose, setting the cup aside. "Come morning, Stella, I want every clock in this house checked. Every staff statement reviewed. We've been chasing ghosts, but someone left fingerprints on the silver."

Stella blinked. "You think it's someone in the household?"

Margot's voice was calm, but firm. "It always is."

And with that, Margot turned back to her desk, the firelight gleaming in her eyes, not from exhaustion, but from renewed determination. She would unravel this knot yet. Not through force, nor luck, but with precision, and patience.

The game was still afoot.

And she intended to win.

_____

14

*T*he morning at Blackwell Manor began with the scent of something faintly acrid drifting through the corridors, curling like a ghost through velvet drapes and mahogany halls. With a practiced air of calm that belied her mounting curiosity, Margot descended the staircase. The scent led her like a trail of invisible ink, guiding her to the garden-facing parlour where the faint orange glow of firelight danced on the walls.

Silhouetted against the hearth, Augustus Lambrook stood like a man caught mid-transgression. His frame was hunched, shoulders tense, and in his hands he held a small stack of paper, which he was steadily feeding into the flames. The flickering light painted him in shifting tones—penitent one moment, defiant the next.

Margot cleared her throat gently, an eyebrow arching in both curiosity and restrained amusement. "A composer at the forge? This is new."

Augustus spun around, visibly startled. A wisp of ash floated free, drifting toward the rug. He attempted a smile, though it wavered dangerously, like the flicker of candlelight in a draught.

"Lady Blackwell," he stammered, his voice low and rasping, "forgive me. I… I couldn't sleep. And these—"

He gestured to the charred remnants in the hearth. "—have no business haunting my desk any longer."

Margot took a measured step closer, the hem of her dressing gown whispering against the rug. Her eyes, ever keen, were fixed on him. "And what, pray, have you condemned to their fiery end?"

Augustus fussed with his collar, taking an instinctive step to shield the fire from view. "Bad reviews," he muttered with a soft, self-deprecating laugh. "Petty critiques from years ago. They seemed significant once, but now…"

He trailed off, shrugging helplessly. The motion was meant to seem casual, but his hand trembled.

Margot tilted her head slightly. "Doubtless, erasing the past has its appeal," she said lightly. "Though it's a curious choice for so early an hour."

"I needed closure," Augustus replied quickly, his smile tightening at the corners. "Bad memories have a way of creeping into one's art."

Margot said nothing, only watching as he fidgeted. Fine grey dust streaked his fingers, and the scent of scorched parchment lingered around him like a shroud. She thought briefly of Evelyn—her talent for manipulation, her hold over Augustus that had been both subtle and savage. Yet, as

Augustus gathered his belongings in a near-panicked shuffle and fled the room, Margot took a step closer to the fireplace.

Among the dying embers, she could just make out the telltale lines of musical notation. They were not editorials or letters; they were compositions.

Margot frowned. Her fingers itched to retrieve them, but the heat and fragility of the ash made the effort futile. Whatever melody Augustus had consigned to smoke, she doubted it would remain silent for long.

———

Later that morning, Margot was seated in the breakfast room, nibbling on a corner of toast and scanning the headlines of a week-old paper, when Stella arrived. She breezed in with the kind of confident informality only a lady's maid with secrets to share could possess.

"I'll give Augustus this much," she announced, dropping a few blackened fragments of paper onto the table before Margot. "He's consistent. Every note's ruined past recognition."

Margot set down her teacup and leaned forward, examining the fragments with interest. "And where, pray, did you find these?"

"Parlour hearth," Stella replied, plopping into the chair opposite. "He's not subtle. The ashes had barely cooled."

Margot picked up one of the pieces, holding it delicately between two fingers. Under the morning light, she could just make out faint, scorched staves and jagged notes. "No bad reviews, then?"

"Unless his critics were classically trained," Stella said dryly. "Seems like he was torching his own work."

Margot set the piece down and brushed her fingers clean. "Escaping the past, by his own admission," she murmured. "Or perhaps cleansing the future."

By midday, Margot's curiosity had fermented into a quiet unease. She took to the gardens to clear her mind, strolling among the roses whose heads bobbed with dew. The stillness of the grounds was deceptive, much like its occupants. The scent of soil and fading petals was almost enough to dull her suspicions.

Almost.

As Margot rounded the corner of the east hedge, she deliberately slowed her pace. Her carefully planned route through the garden had one purpose: to observe Irene Castell without arousing suspicion. Simon had mentioned the young woman had been spotted near the estate's east gate shortly after Evelyn's death, and Margot was determined to discover if that area held any significance.

She feigned surprise when Irene stumbled into view, skirts clutched in one hand and the other cradling a scratched palm.

"Irene," Margot called out, half-amused, half-curious. "Have the roses turned militant?"

Irene froze, then attempted to compose herself. "Lady Blackwell," she said breathlessly. "I... I was gathering a bouquet for Madame Celeste. She's been rather low in spirits."

Margot's expression was neutral, though her eyes flicked to

Irene's scratched hands. "And so you braved the yellow bush at the south gate?"

"I hadn't expected it to be so... defensive," Irene admitted with a sheepish smile. "I thought it'd be quicker if I gathered them myself."

Before Margot could reply, Tom rounded the corner, bearing a tray of tea. He blinked at the scene. "Ah, that explains it! Saw someone struggling with the roses earlier. Took you for the new gardener, Miss Castell."

Irene gave a flustered laugh, nodded quickly, and made a hasty retreat. Margot watched her go.

"She's not very good at lying," came Stella's voice behind her. She emerged from a thicket of rosebush like a cat from the shadows.

"No," Margot agreed. "But sometimes honesty is just better-performed deceit."

———

Back in her study, Margot examined the morning's encounters with a detective's eye. Augustus, allegedly haunted by criticism, had burned what appeared to be a personal composition—his own art sacrificed in secrecy. Irene, scratched and flustered, blamed the roses for a task she could easily have asked a servant to perform. And Tom's innocent observation might've placed her somewhere she shouldn't have been.

The manor was a labyrinth of motives, every hallway echoing with hidden intent. Evelyn Linwood's death remained an unresolved chord, and though the notes scattered around the edges—burnt music, muddied alibis, frayed tempers—they had yet to align into a discernible melody.

Rain began tapping against the windowpanes by late afternoon. Thunder rolled faintly beyond the hills, a promise of storms to come. Margot watched the sky darken, her mind knitting together threads of suspicion, half-truths, and whispered regrets.

As she lit the oil lamp on her desk, a thought struck her: everyone at Blackwell Manor had a secret. Some were merely embarrassing. Others were potentially lethal.

And soon, she would know which was which.

———

Evening fell like a velvet curtain, thick and final. The storm broke just after nightfall. Thunder cracked like a conductor's baton across the sky, and the manor's lights flickered in response. Inside, the walls held their breath.

Margot sat by the fire, the scent of burnt parchment lingering faintly, stubborn as memory. Stella entered quietly, bringing brandy and her usual dry wit.

"Irene's been scrubbing her hands," she said casually. "Like she's trying to erase something more than a thorn scratch."

Margot accepted the glass. "And Augustus?"

"Sulking in the music room," Stella replied. "But not composing. Just… sitting."

The fire snapped sharply in the hearth, and Margot stared into the flames. "We're not far now, Stella. I can feel it. Something's going to give."

"And when it does?"

"Let's hope it plays in tune," Margot said softly.

And with that, the storm outside raged on, but inside, a darker crescendo built. One composed not with instruments but with truths long overdue.

he warm, golden light of the afternoon spilled into Margot's study as she sat before her polished oak writing desk, absently toying with the edge of an unopened envelope. The stillness of the room was broken only by the faint ticking of the clock and the distant hum of activity elsewhere in Blackwell Manor. That relative calm was shattered when Mrs Henshaw appeared in the doorway, looking rather more flustered than usual.

"Lady Blackwell," she began, clasping her hands tightly together. "I beg your pardon, but I've come across something... peculiar."

Margot arched an eyebrow, curiosity piqued. "Peculiar, Mrs Henshaw? At Blackwell Manor, that covers quite a wide range."

Mrs Henshaw hesitated, as though gauging the implication of her discovery before continuing. "It was while I was straightening the guest quarters, ma'am. Specifically, the cabinet in the music room's adjoining dressing area."

"And what did you stumble upon?" Margot asked, rising gracefully from her chair.

Instead of responding, Mrs Henshaw produced a small, battered leather-bound diary and placed it gingerly on Margot's desk. "This," she said curtly, "belongs, or rather belonged, to Miss Evelyn Linwood."

"Where did you find it?" Margot asked, surprised.

"It was tucked behind the loose panel in the music room cabinet—the one that's needed fixing for months. Someone had clearly hidden it there in haste."

Margot turned the diary over in her hands, the worn leather cover giving no hint of its rather explosive contents. She opened it to the first page, where Evelyn's precise and almost aggressively sharp handwriting leapt off the paper. There was no lengthy introduction, no sentimental musings—only a series of enigmatic notations, scribbled like accusations meant for no one but herself.

"J.M.—fraud? A.L.—desperate? I.C.—liar?"

Margot inhaled sharply, her keen eyes scanning further. Each note was curt and cryptic, seemingly tying initials to potential sins. There were references to financial discrepancies, veiled threats of exposure, and tantalising hints at conversations Evelyn had overheard. Yet, never more than initials. It was as though Evelyn had been playing her own private game of chess, each suspect placed strategically on the board, awaiting her next move.

"Cryptic," Stella quipped as she drifted into the room, clearly having overheard the exchange. She peered over Margot's shoulder. "J.M.? Jacques, maybe? So he's suspected of fraud. Not exactly headline news, is it?"

Margot smirked. "Perhaps not, though Evelyn didn't seem prone to documenting trivialities."

Stella leaned closer, her eyes gleaming with curiosity. "And 'A.L.'? Augustus Lambrook. Desperate, is he? Well, we've all seen the man brooding into his soup."

"True, but Evelyn's implications are rarely without basis," Margot said softly, her mind already racing. Finally, she tapped the initials "I.C." with her finger. "Irene Castell, presumably. A liar."

"And a very nervous one, at that," Stella quipped. "This diary's practically a treasure map of grievances."

———

The discussion was interrupted shortly after by Inspector Simon Grant, who swept into the room looking as though he had aged several months in the past few hours. Margot greeted him with a knowing smile. "Ah, Inspector. Perfect timing. Mrs Henshaw has unearthed a rather intriguing artefact."

Simon took the diary, flipping through its pages with characteristic efficiency. "Cryptic enough to remain infuriating," he muttered. Then he stopped mid-page and tapped the faintly scrawled words at the bottom of one entry. *"Outsider?"*

Margot leaned closer, her brow furrowing. "A stranger in the midst of Blackwell Manor?"

Simon nodded. "It's peculiar. It doesn't align with any of our... *residents*. I wonder if Evelyn might have encountered someone beyond these walls."

"And what motive would this alleged stranger carry?" Margot countered. "Evelyn's leverage was inward-facing—Jacques, Augustus, Irene, Celeste. Perhaps this 'outsider' is another red herring."

Simon closed the diary with a soft thud, his expression grim. "Nevertheless, it widens our scope. We can't presume the killer comes purely from within."

"Or perhaps Evelyn's paranoia was merely elaborate," Margot mused.

"Doubtful," Simon countered. "It's been my experience that paranoia is often rooted in truth, even if the truth is clouded."

The debate on Evelyn's diary was cut short when Tom the footman appeared, his usually cheery expression clouded with unease. "Begging your pardon, milady," he said hesitantly, "but Billy's just arrived with news. He says there's talk down at the pub about a stranger asking odd questions about the manor."

Margot's curiosity flared instantly. "Describe this stranger," she commanded.

Tom shifted awkwardly. "Billy didn't get a good look. Said the man kept mostly to himself, but seemed awfully interested in Evelyn and... her connections here."

"How reliable is Billy's account?" Simon interjected.

Tom gave a small shrug. "Reliable enough, sir. Billy's always got his ear to the ground, if you'll forgive the expression."

Margot pursed her lips thoughtfully. "A stranger asking about Evelyn and the manor—coincidence, or something more sinister?"

Simon folded his arms. "If this man exists, and is connected, he's either a witness or another suspect."

"Well," Stella interjected, "if every clue continues pointing in conflicting directions, I say we need more yarn for this tangle."

———

As the evening wore on, Margot found herself in the library once more, piecing together the day's findings. Evelyn's diary had opened an entirely new avenue of suspicion, yet its cryptic nature only served to deepen the mystery. The initials—J.M., A.L., I.C.—each felt damning in its implication, but none provided clear evidence.

And now, on top of it all, the mention of a stranger outside Blackwell Manor added another layer of intrigue. Could it be someone hired by Evelyn's enemies? Or perhaps a ghost from her past revenge-seeking? For all of Evelyn's many talents, keeping her dealings discrete had clearly not been one of them.

Margot leaned back in her chair, staring at the fire crackling in the hearth. Her thoughts turned to Simon's remark about paranoia often being rooted in truth. Evelyn had carefully documented her suspicions about those closest to her, but had she also feared an unnamed force outside the walls of the manor?

The very thought sent a faint shiver down Margot's spine. But she did not allow it to linger long. She would find the answers, no matter how inscrutable the clues—or the players involved.

And somewhere among the initials, accusations, and eerie whispers of strangers in the shadows, lay the key to unravelling the entire mystery of Evelyn Linwood's murder.

16

The air inside Blackwell Manor had grown oppressive, as though the walls themselves were absorbing the tension that had steadily built over the past few days. Even the morning light, which usually danced cheerfully through the grand windows, seemed muted. Margot stood at the edge of the music room, observing the latest attempt at a rehearsal with a sceptical eye. The scene unfolding before her was anything but harmonious.

Augustus Lambrook was seated at the grand piano, his fingers poised awkwardly above the keys. He had always possessed a peculiar, melancholic charm, but today his movements were jerky, uncoordinated, as though an invisible weight pressed down on his shoulders. Irene Castell hovered nervously in the background, clutching a small stack of sheet music as if it were a lifeline. Jacques Maroni, in contrast, leant casually against the mantle, his every gesture exuding his usual air of cavalier indifference.

"Whenever you're ready, Mr Lambrook," Jacques drawled, his voice cutting through the room like a knife through a fraying rope. "Though if you intend to dither for much longer, we may as well clear the room and leave you alone with your inspiration."

Augustus glared at him, his hands clenching into fists. "I *am* trying," he hissed through gritted teeth.

Margot frowned, watching as Augustus suddenly slammed his hands onto the keys, producing a discordant, jarring noise that seemed to echo through the room. He stood abruptly, sending the bench clattering to the floor, and pointed an accusing finger at Jacques.

"She ruined everything!" he shouted, his voice cracking with a mixture of rage and anguish. "Everything I worked for, everything I wanted—she destroyed it all!"

The room fell silent, save for Augustus's ragged breathing. Margot could feel the tension vibrating in the air, sharp and suffocating. She met Stella's wide-eyed gaze from her place near the doorway, her maid's customary sarcasm temporarily wiped away by the sheer drama of the moment.

"Calm yourself, Augustus," Jacques said smoothly, though his composed demeanour was undercut by the faint smirk playing on his lips. He stepped forward slowly, as though approaching a wounded animal. "This outburst isn't helping your case."

"My case?" Augustus spat, his eyes blazing. "Don't pretend you don't know what she was capable of! Evelyn tore people apart for her own amusement. She humiliated me, blackmailed me—"

"She tested you," Jacques interrupted, his voice turning cold. "And she found you wanting."

Margot stiffened at the sharp edge in Jacques's tone. His usual charm had slipped, revealing an undercurrent of menace that sent a shiver down her spine.

The rehearsal dissolved into chaos soon after Augustus's outburst. Jacques, having momentarily adopted the role of pacifier, now stepped into the hallway with Augustus, his voice low and quiet but unmistakably laced with venom. Margot, ever curious, slipped unnoticed into the adjoining corridor and positioned herself out of their sight.

"You're unravelling, Lambrook," Jacques said bluntly. "And if you're not careful, you'll end up implicating yourself in something far worse than your usual pitiful attempts at artistry."

"Is that a threat?" Augustus snapped, his voice trembling with barely contained fury.

"It's a warning," Jacques replied, his tone dangerous. "Don't think I've forgotten your... less savoury exploits. Do you really want those details brought to light? The others might forgive your little transgressions. But the world... you'll never recover."

Margot's fingers tightened against the doorframe. Jacques had always been an unlikeable figure, a man too self-serving to inspire trust, but now she was certain he was far more dangerous than any of them had realised.

———

Later that afternoon, Margot found Irene Castell in the garden, sitting alone on a wrought-iron bench beneath the shade of a sprawling oak tree. Her usually prim appearance was dishevelled; her blonde hair slightly out of place, and her hands wringing a handkerchief with nervous energy. Margot approached quietly, taking a seat beside her.

"Irene," she began gently, "you seem troubled."

Irene glanced at her, her lips pressed into a tight line. "It's nothing, Lady Blackwell. Just… everything feels so heavy."

"I've been meaning to ask, Irene," Margot began, her voice delicate yet probing, "how it was you came to be in Madame Celeste's employ."

Irene looked down, her shoulders tensed. "It wasn't the life I imagined for myself," she admitted softly, a pained smile gracing her lips. "I came to London dreaming of theatreland. I aspired to be a musician, you see, a pianist, and I thought ambition alone would open the doors."

Margot's curiosity piqued. "But ambition only takes one so far," she said gently, sensing there was more to the story.

Irene nodded, her fingers nervously twisting at the seam of her dress. "I faced rejection after rejection. No one wanted to take a chance on me—not for concerts, not for plays. I was ready to give up everything when Madame Celeste found me playing in a dingy pub, surviving on pennies and dreams."

Her eyes filled with unexpected tears. "She took me in when no one else would. Gave me purpose, dignity… a future. You can't understand what that means. To have nothing, to be nothing, and then suddenly to matter to someone like her. I would do anything for her. Anything."

Margot's brows lifted. "She saw something in you?"

"She recognised my passion," Irene replied, her voice breaking slightly. "She didn't offer me the stage, but she gave me work as her assistant. It wasn't the dream I'd pictured, but at least I was close to music, close to the life I yearned for. For that, I will always be grateful to her."

An almost reverent silence stretched between them, broken only by the faint sound of the wind stirring the flowers in the garden. For the first time, Margot saw not the trembling assistant but a woman weighed down by dreams worn thin.

"Everything feels different now," Irene said, her voice catching as she gazed out toward the sky. "It's as though Evelyn's shadow remains, judging everything I do and everything I couldn't."

"You're not alone in that," Margot said, her voice soft but measured. "It seems this house has drawn us all into its web."

Irene hesitated, then sighed. "Do you think—" She broke off, biting her lip. "Do you think everyone here is capable of such things? Of murder, I mean?"

Margot took a moment to consider her response. "I think," she said carefully, "that desperation makes people do unimaginable things. And secrecy only sharpens that desperation."

Irene nodded slowly, her gaze fixed on a patch of sunlight filtering through the leaves. "I just... I fear everyone will think the worst of us, no matter who did it."

Margot could hear the tremor in her voice, the vulnerability slipping through her usually guarded exterior. "And who is 'us'?" Margot asked, her curiosity piqued.

Irene looked at her sharply, but whatever response she might have given was interrupted by the sudden arrival of Tom, who came bounding down the garden path with a clumsy kind of energy that was both endearing and exasperating.

"Begging your pardon, milady," he said breathlessly, "but the inspector's looking for you."

"Of course he is," Margot said with a sigh. Turning back to Irene, she offered a faint smile. "We'll finish this conversation later, Miss Castell."

Irene nodded, her expression unreadable, as Margot rose and followed Tom toward the manor.

———

Back in the study, Simon spread his notes across Margot's desk, creating a timeline of events.

"Look here," he said, pointing to a particular entry. "Evelyn was seen arguing with Jacques at 7 pm. Augustus claims he was composing in his room until 9 pm, but Mrs Henshaw heard the piano silent after 8. Irene says she was with Celeste all evening, yet Mary saw her in the kitchen at 8:30. And the doctor places the time of death between 8 and 10 pm."

He drew lines connecting various notes. "I'm looking for the overlap—the moment when opportunity, means, and motive converge. Someone slipped away, someone lied about their whereabouts, someone had access to that piano wire."

Margot watched him work, impressed by the methodical precision of his mind. "You see patterns where others see chaos," she observed.

Simon looked up, a rare smile crossing his features. "It's not so different from your approach, Lady Blackwell. We're both looking for the discord in the symphony."

"I'm starting to wonder," Margot mused, "if the key to all this isn't who killed Evelyn, but why."

Simon nodded slowly, his expression thoughtful. "Motive," he said quietly. "That's the one element no one's willing to discuss."

"Not openly," Margot corrected, a faint smile tugging at her lips. "But secrets have a way of revealing themselves. And I suspect that if we keep pressing, something or someone will finally snap."

17

_____

The morning light streamed softly through the tall windows of Blackwell Manor, painting long golden ribbons across the parquet floor. Dust motes danced in the sunbeams, suspended in the hush that only old, brooding houses seem to know. On any other day, such light might have seemed warm, almost cheerful. But today, it felt like a cruel deception, a delicate veil cast over an atmosphere thick with suspicion and unease.

Margot, ever composed, sat alone in the breakfast room, her coffee cooling in its porcelain cup. The scent of toast, fresh butter, and her usual French-pressed brew lingered in the air, but she hardly noticed. Her mind was already half-occupied with the events of the past week. Evelyn Linwood's tragic and sudden death had upended life at the manor, and each new day brought with it another whisper of intrigue.

The heavy oak door creaked open, and Mrs Henshaw stepped in with her customary precision. Her starched apron was immaculate, her steel-grey hair coiled tightly at the nape of her neck. Yet today, something in her bearing was off, her movements just a shade too brisk, her expression a fraction too taut.

"Lady Blackwell," she began, dipping her head slightly, "I do apologise for the interruption. During my morning inspection, I came across something... rather unusual in Madame Celeste's dressing room."

Margot looked up, her interest immediately piqued. She set her cup down with care and folded her hands neatly in her lap. "Unusual, Mrs Henshaw? Do elaborate."

Mrs Henshaw took a measured breath. "A pair of gloves, ma'am. Fine leather, quite new. But what caught my eye was the peculiar residue on the fingertips. A sort of metallic sheen. I found them placed neatly on the table by her looking glass. They were not there yesterday."

Margot's brow furrowed slightly. "Metallic residue, you say? Curious indeed. Could it be paint, perhaps? Or something more industrial?"

"I couldn't say for certain, milady," Mrs Henshaw replied. "But the substance glinted under the morning light. I thought it best not to disturb them further without your guidance."

"You were right to come to me," Margot said, rising with the quiet poise she always carried, even under pressure. "If there's anything unusual about these gloves, they may well prove significant. Come, we shall retrieve them immediately."

They stepped out into the corridor, the long gallery lined with ancestral portraits watching their every move with cold, oil-painted eyes. Blackwell Manor seemed to hold its breath.

As they rounded the corner near the east wing, the pair encountered Inspector Simon Grant, looking uncharacteristically dishevelled. His coat was unbuttoned, his hair slightly mussed, and he was chewing the end of a pen with a thoughtful ferocity that suggested he hadn't slept much.

"Lady Blackwell," he greeted, sounding only half-present. "You're out early. Heading somewhere specific?"

Margot stopped, her expression unreadable. "Indeed, Inspector. Mrs Henshaw has discovered a pair of gloves in Madame Celeste's dressing room. She described a curious metallic residue on the fingers."

That brought Simon fully into the moment. He straightened, tucking the pen into his jacket pocket. "Metallic residue? That's rather intriguing. Trace evidence, perhaps. Paint, rust... or blood. Could be crucial."

"Quite," Margot said, her eyes glinting. "We were just going to inspect them."

"I'll accompany you," Simon said at once, falling into step beside them. "The more eyes, the better."

As they made their way down the corridor, Margot noted a subtle change in Mrs Henshaw's demeanour. There was a stiffness in her stride, an unspoken tension that suggested more than just concern over a pair of gloves. Something gnawed at her, though she said nothing.

When they reached Madame Celeste's chambers, Mrs Henshaw raised a hand and knocked briskly. "Madame? It's Mrs Henshaw. Might we enter?"

There was a pause, followed by the faint, lilting voice of Celeste drifting through the door. "Do come in."

Inside, the room was as dramatically styled as its occupant; plush fabrics, heavy perfumes, and mirrored surfaces everywhere. Celeste sat before her vanity, brushing her golden curls with slow, deliberate strokes. The soft rustle of satin accompanied her movements.

She glanced up into the mirror as they entered. Her eyes flicked over each face, and her expression settled into a blend of mild curiosity and slight irritation. "Lady Blackwell. Inspector Grant. Mrs Henshaw. This feels delightfully official."

"Madame," Margot began evenly, "Mrs Henshaw discovered a pair of gloves in this room earlier this morning. She found them resting on the table by your looking glass. The gloves were described as having a metallic residue on the fingers."

Celeste blinked, then slowly set her brush down, her long fingers curling around the handle as if reluctant to let go. "Gloves? I own several. You'll have to be more specific."

"They were on that table," Mrs Henshaw said, pointing toward a small side table beside the wardrobe.

All eyes turned.

The table was empty except for a silver candlestick and a neatly folded lace-edged handkerchief.

No gloves.

"Gone," Margot said simply, though a note of steel had crept into her tone.

Simon stepped forward and crouched beside the table, inspecting its surface. He rubbed two fingers lightly along the polished wood, then sniffed them, as though expecting to catch a whiff of whatever substance had once coated the gloves.

"Are you absolutely certain, Mrs Henshaw?" he asked, though the question was merely procedural. His expression said he already believed her.

"Without a doubt," she replied firmly. "I saw them not two hours ago."

Celeste reclined slightly in her chair, crossing her legs at the ankle. "I'm afraid I haven't the faintest idea what gloves you're referring to," she said with airy disinterest. "Perhaps one of the maids moved them while dusting. Things do tend to get shifted about."

Margot studied Celeste with keen eyes. Beneath the feigned indifference, there was something—something small and quick and tight around the corners of her mouth. A flicker of tension. A tell.

"You must understand," Margot said, her voice silky, "that this isn't merely about missing gloves. If the residue is what we suspect, the gloves could be central to our investigation."

"I see." Celeste smiled, though it lacked warmth. "And if they are so very important, I do hope you find them quickly. I'd hate for such evidence to go astray in this great, drafty house."

Simon straightened, rubbing his temple with one hand. "Wandering gloves don't inspire confidence in the security of a crime scene," he muttered.

Margot placed a calming hand on his arm. "We'll see to locating them, Inspector."

She turned back to Celeste, who was once again running her brush through her curls as if nothing had happened. "Thank you for your time, Madame. If the gloves happen to reappear, I trust you'll let us know at once?"

"But of course," Celeste purred. "Anything to assist."

Margot's gaze drifted to the window, where a cool breeze rustled the ivy climbing along the manor's walls. Her expression softened as memories flickered behind her eyes.

"There was a time when this place was simply home, a backdrop to a carefree life I thought would last forever. But when I lost my parents—too soon, too suddenly—it became more than that. Overnight, Blackwell Manor was no longer just bricks and mortar; it was my responsibility." She paused, her lips curling faintly. "I admit, at first, the weight of it was overwhelming. But now... I'm its custodian, and I wouldn't have it any other way. My duty is to protect its peace."

Once back in the corridor, Simon let out a low growl of frustration. "Gone. Just like that. Either we're dealing with a compulsive cleaner or someone's deliberately covering their tracks."

Margot folded her arms, her brow furrowed in thought. "Celeste plays the innocent well, but she overplays her hand. That brush, the pose, the affected nonchalance—it was too carefully curated."

Simon nodded. "She's hiding something. Whether it's the gloves or something deeper remains to be seen."

"She's not the only one who had access to that room," Margot said quietly. "Any number of staff might have passed through this morning. We'll need to question them. Discreetly."

"And the residue?" Simon asked. "What do you suspect it might be?"

Margot didn't answer right away. Her mind was already sorting through possibilities. Gunmetal? Mercury? Graphite? Something from the stables or the old smithy? Whatever it was, someone clearly didn't want it found.

"We'll start by speaking with Stella," she said finally. "She was assigned to Celeste this week, wasn't she?"

Mrs Henshaw, still with them, gave a firm nod. "Yes, milady. Stella's been attending to Madame Celeste since Miss Linwood's passing. She would know if anything was moved."

"Then let's not waste time," Margot said.

As they moved toward the servants' wing, Margot's heels tapping a steady rhythm on the stone floor; a troubling thought lingered in her mind.

Evidence had a strange way of vanishing at Blackwell Manor. Just when something solid seemed within reach, it slipped through their fingers like sand. The gloves, once an unexpected boon, had now joined the ranks of other secrets that skulked in the shadows of the house.

But Margot was no stranger to shadows.

And she was determined to drag this mystery into the light.

18

---

*T*he investigation had reached that frustrating stage where evidence had been gathered but conclusions remained elusive. Something was missing—a connection, a motive strong enough to drive someone to murder. Her thoughts were interrupted by a commotion in the hallway.

Margot had instructed Mrs Henshaw to have the staff search every linen closet and storage area; a directive that raised eyebrows but which she insisted was necessary. "If someone wished to hide evidence," she'd explained, "they'd choose a place both accessible and overlooked."

Her strategy proved correct when Mary's voice echoed through the corridors. "Lady Blackwell! I've found something!"

The linen basket had been Margot's suggestion specifically— she'd noticed Irene hovering near it the previous evening, supposedly straightening linens but perhaps concealing something more damning.

Margot looked up just as her lady's maid, Stella, swept in with a curious glint in her eye.

"Well, milady," Stella said, with a tone that suggested she was restraining laughter, "I do hope you're seated comfortably."

Margot arched a brow. "I am. Should I not be?"

Stella gave a theatrical sigh. "The gloves have reappeared."

Margot closed her book at once. "The gloves?"

"The very same. Turned up just now in the linen basket." She folded her arms. "Mary found them, naturally. Caused quite the stir below stairs."

Margot rose, placing her cup gently on the side table. "The linen basket? That's hardly where one misplaces fine leather gloves, especially not ones potentially tied to a murder."

"Quite," Stella agreed. "Unless someone wanted them to disappear… and then *reappear*."

Together, they moved swiftly through the house, the sense of urgency beneath Margot's composed stride mirrored in Stella's quick step. The linen closet was a narrow alcove near the servants' wing, lined with shelves of folded linens and a large wicker basket meant for clean sheets waiting to be returned to the guest rooms. When they arrived, half a dozen staff were already gathered, forming a loose semicircle around the basket, their expressions ranging from intrigue to alarm.

Mrs Henshaw was front and centre, her hands on her hips and her voice ringing through the space with characteristic authority.

"You've been told to be *vigilant!*" she scolded, glaring at the younger maids as though their mere presence offended her.

"This is not a barnyard. It is Blackwell Manor, and we are not in the habit of misplacing clues!"

Mary, one of the youngest maids, stood red-faced and flustered beside the basket, wringing her hands. "But I didn't put them there!" she insisted, her copper hair escaping from beneath her cap. "I was fetching linens for the south bedroom, and there they were, just... sitting on top!"

"And I suppose they flew in of their own accord?" Mrs Henshaw snapped. "Heaven preserve us from such foolishness."

Margot stepped forward, her calm voice cutting through the rising tension. "That's enough. Let's not point fingers without cause."

The group parted respectfully as Margot approached the basket. There, among layers of crisp, white linens, lay the gloves—fine, dove-grey leather, elegant and unmistakable. One glove rested atop the other, the fingers curled as though they had been gently placed there by an unseen hand.

With delicate precision, Margot reached for them, lifting them free. The strange, dark metallic residue still clung to the fingertips, catching the lamplight in odd ways. She turned them over in her hands, frowning.

They were just as Mrs Henshaw had described earlier that morning—yet their sudden reappearance raised more questions than answers.

"Mary," Margot said gently, "you're quite certain they were here when you opened the basket?"

The girl nodded furiously. "I swear it, milady. I pulled back the top sheet and saw them straightaway. I didn't touch them. I ran to fetch Mrs Henshaw right off."

"I should hope so," Mrs Henshaw muttered. "This entire ordeal has been an embarrassment."

Margot suppressed a sigh and addressed the gathered staff. "Regardless of how they came to be here, these gloves will be kept under secure watch. Until we understand their role in all this, no one is to touch them. Am I clear?"

A chorus of solemn nods followed, and slowly, the staff began to drift away, their murmured speculations trailing behind them like smoke. Only Mrs Henshaw remained, arms still crossed, her brow furrowed with simmering displeasure.

"I don't like it, milady," she said quietly, once the others had gone. "It feels… wrong. As though someone's playing games."

Margot regarded her with careful eyes. "Yes," she agreed. "And I intend to find out who."

———

Later that evening, the wind had risen outside, brushing against the tall windows of the dining room with a low, mournful sigh, as though Blackwell Manor itself were weary of its secrets. The long table, now cleared of supper, stretched like a polished lane between candelabras. Margot sat at its head, her figure elegant and composed in the flickering glow of the tapers.

Before her, resting on a folded linen napkin rather than silk, lay the gloves—quiet, damning, inexplicably returned. She turned one over gently, her fingers moving with a curious reverence, as if the leather might murmur something—an echo of violence, a whisper of guilt.

Her mind drifted, unbidden, to Evelyn Linwood. Beautiful, vivacious Evelyn, with her quick smile and quicker secrets.

Her death had not merely disturbed the household; it had unsettled its very foundations. These gloves, pristine yet sinister, might have gripped the very instrument of her murder. They might belong to the person who had extinguished that bright spark of life.

The silence was broken by a soft rap at the door leading from the hallway.

"Come in," Margot called, not taking her eyes off the gloves.

Inspector Simon Grant stepped inside, the candlelight casting lean shadows across his overcoat and tired face. He looked like a man who had walked through too many dusk-lit corridors with too few answers.

"You asked to see me, Lady Blackwell?"

Margot gestured to the end of the table, where the gloves lay like some relic from a darker age. "They've returned," she said simply.

Simon's brows knit together. "Returned?"

"In the linen basket," she said with a dry smile. "Mary claims she found them while gathering the table linens."

Simon approached, his footfalls soft against the carpeted floor. He leaned forward, careful not to touch the gloves, his eyes narrowing.

"But that corridor was under watch," he muttered. "I assigned a constable after our last visit to Celeste's rooms."

Margot allowed herself a cool sip of tea before replying. "Then perhaps your constable has a blind spot. Or someone knew just when to take advantage of it."

Simon shook his head, grim. "If they were taken, then returned… that's no accident. It's measured. Someone isn't frightened, they're playing a game."

Margot rose slowly, moving to stand beside him. "And if it's a game, then the gloves are a move. A calculated one."

He crouched to examine the residue clinging faintly to the fingertips. "Still here," he murmured. "Untouched. Odd. Most people would have tried to wipe it off."

"Unless they wanted us to see it," Margot said, her tone thoughtful. "To be led somewhere. Or away from something."

He stood again, gaze never leaving the gloves. "This isn't panic. It's precision. Someone wants to muddy the timeline, stir doubt, confuse us about where the gloves have been and when."

Margot nodded slowly. "Evelyn would have seen through it in an instant. She had a talent for sniffing out falsehoods."

Simon's expression softened for a moment, a flicker of sympathy crossing his features. "She was clever. Too clever for her own good, perhaps."

Silence stretched between them, broken only by the wind worrying at the leaded panes and the faint creak of the chandeliers overhead.

Finally, Margot asked, "Do you think the gloves are a warning?"

Simon considered this, his arms folded. "No. If they meant to frighten us, they'd have done more. No—this is misdirection. Someone wants our eyes elsewhere. The real question is, what don't they want us to see?"

Margot exhaled softly, her gaze drifting to the far end of the dining room where portraits of long-dead Blackwells hung in heavy gilt frames, their painted eyes forever watching.

"Then we mustn't be drawn in," she said. "We'll look where they hope we won't. Evelyn deserves at least that."

Simon gave a single nod. "Agreed. I'll send the gloves to forensics tonight. We need to know exactly what's on them—paint, powder, perhaps something more telling. And if we're lucky, there may be fingerprints. Though I won't count on it."

He pulled a small wooden box from the satchel at his side, padded inside with straw. Carefully, he placed the gloves within and sealed the lid shut with brisk efficiency.

"I'll have a constable collect them before midnight," he added. "And I'll speak with the station chemist myself."

Margot stepped back, watching the gloves disappear into the shadows of the box. "It's strange, isn't it?" she murmured. "That something so elegant could be so thoroughly menacing."

"It always is," Simon replied, tucking the box under his arm. "Murder tends to wear a charming face until the moment it strikes."

He turned to go, pausing only briefly at the door. "Rest if you can. Tomorrow, we'll start again with sharper eyes."

After he left, the hush in the dining room seemed to deepen. Margot remained standing for a moment, staring at the place the gloves had rested. The tapers flickered, their flames disturbed by a draft none of the servants could ever find, and somewhere beyond the heavy curtains, the storm muttered over the moors.

She crossed to the window and pulled the drapes aside. Beyond the frost-laced glass, the gardens were swallowed in mist and moonlight, the hedgerows still as grave markers.

Someone out there knew the truth. Someone who moved through Blackwell Manor like a shadow, careful, quiet, cruel. But truth had a way of bleeding through the cracks, no matter how tightly they were sealed.

She laid a hand on the cold windowpane and whispered, so low even the storm couldn't carry it away:

"I will find you. No matter where you hide."

And with that vow, she turned from the night and returned to the glowing hearth, where the warmth could not quite banish the chill coiled deep in her bones.

19

The evening light in Blackwell Manor's grand dining room shifted with quiet grace, filtering through tall, mullioned windows and casting lattice-like shadows across the gleaming table. The scent of beeswax polish still lingered faintly in the air, and the clink of a silver sugar spoon in porcelain teacups punctuated the otherwise heavy silence.

Margot sat at the far end of the table, her spine straight and her expression composed, though drawn taut with tension. Opposite her, Inspector Simon Grant leaned forward with his usual unyielding focus, his notebook open and a pen tapping a quiet, impatient rhythm against the page. He had returned to Blackwell Manor not long ago, having personally ensured that the gloves bearing residue were sent off to forensics. Now, the table between them stretched like a polished battlefield, one side cloaked in aristocratic poise, the other armed with dogged inquiry.

"I can't make sense of it," Simon muttered, the tap of his pen quickening. "The gloves vanish before we can send them to forensics. Then they miraculously reappear, in a laundry basket, of all places. The same gloves with a metallic residue that might connect to Evelyn's death. And Celeste, always flitting between cryptic and incoherent."

Margot set down her teacup with practiced calm, her eyes cool and calculating. "Misplacement is never innocent at Blackwell, Simon. Every lost object is a deliberate move. The house is being played like a game board."

Simon looked up. "You think someone in this house is orchestrating the chaos?"

"I think someone wants us constantly three steps behind," she replied. "Every clue we chase leads us in circles. It's a tapestry of misdirection, and someone is quite skilled at weaving it."

Before Simon could respond, a low groan rumbled from above, a prolonged, almost organic sound, like a great beast shifting in its sleep. Margot's eyes flicked upward. Then came the unmistakable creak of strained metal.

"Move!" Simon shouted.

He was on his feet in an instant, grabbing Margot's arm and pulling her sharply to the side. Their chairs skidded back just as a thunderous *crack* tore through the room.

A heartbeat later, the grand chandelier, a glittering beast of crystal and brass, plummeted from the ceiling and crashed down onto the long dining table. The sound was deafening. Splinters of wood, shards of glass, and curls of twisted metal erupted in every direction. Dust billowed through the air like smoke from a cannon, and then, all was still.

Margot coughed lightly, brushing a splinter from her sleeve. Her heartbeat thudded in her ears, but she stood tall, unshaken. "Well," she said dryly, surveying the wreckage, "that's certainly one way to clear a room."

Simon was already crouched near the mangled fixture, inspecting the damage with narrowed eyes. "This wasn't decay or misfortune," he said grimly. "The chain's been tampered with."

Servants soon flooded into the dining room, drawn by the commotion. Mrs Henshaw arrived first, barking orders even before she crossed the threshold.

"Clear this immediately! Mind the glass! Oh, heavens above, look at this mess—what in the devil happened?"

"Sabotage," Simon said curtly, still kneeling. "And nearly successful."

Margot nodded in agreement, her eyes scanning the watching staff. "Whoever did this wanted to send a message."

———

By late afternoon the next day, whispers had taken root like ivy through the manor's corridors. Blackwell's staff spoke in hurried, hushed voices behind closed doors. Tom, the young footman, hovered uncertainly near the dining room threshold, his complexion pale and nervous energy radiating from every fidget.

"Tom," Margot said sharply, beckoning him forward with a glance. "You've something to say, haven't you?"

Tom stepped into the ruined room, his hands clenched into fists. "It weren't meant to happen like this," he muttered. "I... I only meant to help, milady."

Simon stood. "Help with what, exactly?"

Tom's voice cracked under the weight of fear. "Last week, I saw the chandelier chain looked worn. I thought if I waited and it broke… well, I'd be blamed. So I tried to fix it meself."

Margot arched a brow. "With what?"

"A bit of wire I found upstairs," he said. "In one of Mr Lambrook's trunks. It looked strong. Good quality. I swear I didn't mean for anything bad to happen."

Simon's tone hardened. "You used unverified material on a four-hundred-pound chandelier? Without telling anyone?"

Tom looked stricken. "I thought I was doing the right thing… truly, I did."

Margot was livid at this bit of new revelation but her voice was level. "What business did you have in Mr Lambrook's trunks, Tom?"

Silence.

"What else did you see in Mr Lambrook's trunk?" she asked.

"Mostly music things. Strings, cases… but sometimes tools. Things to fix instruments, I suppose."

Simon rubbed his jaw. "Or sabotage household fixtures."

Tom paled further. "No, sir! Mr Lambrook didn't know I took it! He didn't know!"

"We'll see about that," Margot murmured. "Simon, I think it's time we paid Mr Lambrook a visit."

———

The drawing room was dim when they entered, golden light slanting through the windows, catching the dust motes in the air. Augustus Lambrook reclined in a velvet chair near the hearth, a music book open in his lap. He looked up, faintly irritated by the interruption.

"Come to interrogate me again, have you?" he asked, closing the book with a snap.

Margot ignored the sarcasm. "Your trunk, Mr Lambrook— Tom claims to have borrowed wire from it to repair the chandelier."

Augustus frowned. "What on earth was he doing rummaging through my belongings?"

Simon stepped forward. "Did you give him permission?"

"Of course not!" Augustus replied indignantly. "Why would I? I didn't even know anything was missing."

Margot watched him closely. "Then you won't object if we examine the contents of your trunks."

A flicker of hesitation crossed his face. "Fine. If it clears my name, search away. You'll find nothing."

"We'll be the judge of that," Simon said.

The trunks in Augustus's quarters were neatly packed. Sheet music, rosin, spare bowstrings, and indeed, coils of wire— some heavy, some thin and delicate. Simon examined the wire spools with gloved hands.

"This one's half-used," he said, lifting it. "Could match the chandelier repair."

"No fingerprints on the wire," Augustus muttered. "Not unless you've brought a magician."

"We'll take it anyway," Simon replied. "And your cooperation is... noted."

————

Evening fell like a velvet curtain over Blackwell, and the manor seemed to hold its breath. The remnants of the chandelier had been cleared, but its absence left the dining room feeling hollow and strange. In the parlour, Margot and Simon regrouped, both wearied by the day's descent into chaos.

As they sat in uneasy silence, the door opened, and in swept Jacques Maroni, trailing his usual scent of expensive cologne and flamboyant disinterest.

"I come bearing sympathy," he announced. "And perhaps a touch of scandalous gossip."

"You always do," Margot murmured, not looking up.

Simon regarded him wearily. "And where were you when the ceiling nearly collapsed on our heads?"

Jacques arched a brow. "Teaching, of course. West wing. Group rehearsal. Ask Mary and Betsy, they'll vouch for me."

Simon didn't even flinch. "We already have."

"Then what do you want from me?" Jacques asked, spreading his arms. "A confession I don't possess?"

Margot glanced at him. "Just the truth. When you're ready to part with it."

Jacques tilted his head. "Ah, Lady Blackwell. So elegant, so biting. But the truth? It's slippery, no? Like a violin string too tightly wound, ready to snap."

"And when it does?" Simon asked.

Jacques smiled enigmatically. "Then we'll all hear the music."

Later, in the dim dining room, now eerily quiet without the chandelier's presence, Margot stood beside the long table, her gloved hand trailing over the polished surface. The room had once been a haven for meals and conversations, but now it bore the memory of shattering glass and unseen danger.

Simon re-entered, holding a sealed evidence pouch.

"The gloves are now with forensics," he said. "We'll see what the residue reveals. Paint? Chemicals? Something more telling, perhaps. And if the gods are kind, we may get fingerprints this time."

Margot looked at him thoughtfully. "You still believe it's all a distraction?"

"I do," Simon replied. "The gloves, the chandelier, Lambrook's tools—it's all to keep us chasing ghosts while the real story hides in plain sight."

He paused, lowering his voice. "Jacques Maroni's finances show transfers to Swiss banks that coincide perfectly with Evelyn's blackmail timeline. He had motive, opportunity, and the theatrical knowledge to stage such a dramatic end. I've seen killers like him before—men who believe themselves above consequence, who eliminate problems with the same ease they sign contracts."

Margot turned to the darkened windows. The garden paths were silvered by moonlight, frost edging the glass like lace.

"Then we must look harder," she said softly. "Because Evelyn

Linwood deserves the truth, however deeply buried it may be."

Simon gave a short nod. "And we'll find it. Even if we have to dig through every secret this house holds."

As they left the room, the light from the hall spilled in behind them—casting long shadows across the floor. Blackwell Manor, silent once more, seemed to exhale. But its secrets remained rooted in the walls, waiting.

And somewhere in its depths, the truth watched and waited too.

20

*M*argot, ever the patient observer and mistress of discretion, moved with quiet grace through the east wing, having intended to take the long path to the west garden for her usual hour of reflection. But as she passed the narrow corridor leading toward the guest quarters, a subtle, acrid scent lingered in the air. Her steps slowed. Smoke. Faint but unmistakable. Not the pleasant aroma of a fireplace fed with seasoned oak, but something sharper—more deliberate. Burning paper.

Her brow furrowed, curiosity piqued. Rather than summon one of the staff, she followed the trail herself, each step quieter than the last. The smell grew stronger, curling through the air like a warning. It led her unmistakably to the private quarters of Jacques Maroni.

The Frenchman was a man of refined charm and hidden calculations, always impeccably dressed and effortlessly aloof. But as Margot reached his door, the squeal of a floorboard beneath her shoe betrayed her arrival. Within, the scene was telling.

Jacques, usually a paragon of nonchalance, was crouched before the hearth like a man caught in a compromising act. He looked up sharply, his dark eyes flashing with something unspoken. In his hands were several sheets of paper, some already half-consumed by flame. The fire crackled louder than usual, as if feeding on secrets rather than wood.

"Well," Margot drawled, her voice calm and cool, "this is certainly an interesting sight."

Jacques, caught between defiance and embarrassment, straightened slowly. His usual smirk formed, but it lacked conviction. "Lady Blackwell," he said smoothly, brushing imaginary soot from his cuffs. "You assume far too much of a man merely purging the remnants of correspondence past. Clutter, nothing more."

Margot stepped into the room, arms folding neatly across her bodice. "Letters?" she asked, her tone light but laced with meaning. "That must be some mighty clutter, to deserve the cleansing flame."

Before Jacques could craft a retort, another presence made itself known. The unmistakable clack of boot heels on polished wood heralded the arrival of Inspector Simon Grant. Always just a pace or two behind Margot in these matters, the inspector's mood was never improved by the fact.

He paused in the doorway, brow furrowed, then took in the scene with a sigh. "What's this now?" he asked briskly. "Burning evidence, Jacques?"

Jacques turned toward him, that same smile still fixed in place, though it had begun to slip at the corners. "I assure you, Inspector, there is nothing of evidentiary value here.

Old debts. Letters from creditors. Hardly the stuff of intrigue."

Simon's eyes narrowed. "And yet," he said, voice dry as dust, "you felt compelled to reduce them to ash rather than drop them in a wastebasket like a civilised man."

"Some memories are better erased than stored," Jacques replied smoothly, holding up a half-scorched envelope with a theatrical flourish. "Besides, you wouldn't want your guest rooms littered with unsightly clutter, would you?"

Margot tilted her head, her gaze sharp. "And tell me, Jacques, do these letters contain more than just overdue bills? Regrets, perhaps? Or secrets better left unread?"

He met her gaze, the firelight flickering in his eyes. "If I had secrets, milady, rest assured they would not be committed to paper."

Simon stepped forward, adjusting his hat with a deliberate motion. "Burning things during an active investigation is hardly wise, Maroni. Keep the rest of your papers intact, or I'll be forced to consider it obstruction."

Jacques inclined his head in mock deference. "Of course, Inspector."

But Margot was not finished. She studied him, noting the tautness in his jaw, the faint tremble in one of his fingers as it brushed soot from his sleeve. "The question," she said, voice silken, "is not what you're hiding, Jacques, but why you so often feel the need to."

There was a flicker—barely visible, but there—a crack in the mask he wore so well. But before he could answer, Margot turned, satisfied. "Come, Simon. We've other matters more deserving of our time than Monsieur Maroni's pyrotechnics."

She swept from the room, skirts whispering along the floor. Simon cast Jacques one last withering look before following.

———

Later that day, with the scent of burnt paper still clinging faintly to her senses, Margot found herself in the back hallway near the kitchens. The scent here was more pleasant —lavender soap and freshly baked bread. But the conversation to come would be no less combustible.

Irene Castell, young and nervy, stood overseeing the preparation of Madame Celeste's midday tea tray. She was checking the arrangement of petit fours with obsessive precision, her fingers fluttering like nervous birds.

"Irene," Margot said, stepping into the light. Her tone was warm, almost kind, but held the weight of expectation.

Irene froze, then turned slowly. "Lady Blackwell," she said, offering a quick curtsy. "Inspector Grant."

Simon nodded curtly, arms folded.

"What can you tell us about your whereabouts the other night?" Margot asked gently. "When the chandelier fell?"

Irene's fingers tightened ever so slightly around the silver tray. "I wasn't in the dining room," she said quickly. "I was in the scullery—fetching hot water for Madame Celeste. She gets cramps in her hands after supper."

"Convenient," Simon murmured, eyes narrowing.

"It's the truth," Irene said, firmer now. "And after that, I went to mend a tear in my bedroom's drapes which Mrs Henshaw had brought to my attention earlier that day."

Margot regarded her in silence. Irene stood perfectly still, save for the faint quiver of her tray. Her eyes held no defiance, only wide-eyed fear—and something else, perhaps: the desperate hope that the truth would be enough.

"We shall confirm it," Margot said at last. "You may return to your duties, Miss Castell."

Irene dipped in a low, unsteady curtsy, then turned and hurried off down the corridor, the soft clink of silver her only farewell.

Simon exhaled through his nose. "If her alibi holds, and I think it might, then we can strike her from the list."

Margot nodded.

"That leaves Jacques," Simon said grimly. "And Augustus. Our resident recluse."

Margot's expression darkened. "Yes," she murmured. "And I can't help but feel we're circling a truth still cloaked in smoke."

———

That evening, as twilight settled like a velvet shawl across the estate, the manor took on an entirely different quality. Gone was the golden afternoon light; in its place, the hallways were hushed, dimly lit by flickering sconces. The wind murmured against the windows. Somewhere in the distance, a servant closed a door too forcefully.

In her study, Margot sat beside the fire, the flames casting shifting patterns across her thoughtful face. Across from her, in her usual armchair, sat Stella, her lady's maid and confidante, who twirled the corner of a cushion absentmindedly.

"Well," Stella said, her voice light but tinged with exasperation, "you've certainly made your rounds today. Caught Jacques with his secret inferno, interrogated poor Irene over a scullery visit, though I suspect that part was more Simon's doing than yours."

Margot allowed herself a smile. "I only asked questions. Irene answered."

"And still," Stella continued, "we're no closer to solving anything. Evelyn Linwood is still dead, everyone has something to hide, and we have more suspects than the London Opera has sopranos."

Margot leaned back, letting the firelight flicker across her eyes. "Perhaps," she said quietly, "but each day, each conversation, chips away at the façade. We'll get there."

Stella frowned. "It's a peculiar thing, isn't it? This house. Always full of whispers and glances. Ever since Evelyn's death, it feels like Blackwell Manor itself is holding its breath."

Margot didn't answer immediately. She let the silence settle between them, thoughtful and heavy. Then she said, "Everyone's hiding something. Some secrets are harmless. But others... fester. Jacques burns his letters. Augustus locks himself away. Even Celeste watches everything, as if from a distance."

Stella arched a brow. "And what about you, milady? Do you have secrets worth burning?"

Margot gave a rare laugh, low and warm. "Oh, certainly. But

I prefer mine carefully catalogued, just in case I need to retrieve them."

They sat in companionable silence for a while, broken only by the soft crackle of the hearth. Outside, the night thickened. Somewhere in the distance, an owl called, mournful and lonesome.

At last, Stella stood and stretched. "If you ask me," she said, smoothing her skirts, "whoever did it is counting on us chasing our tails. But they've underestimated you, milady."

Margot's eyes, sharp and gleaming, lifted to meet hers. "And Inspector Grant," she added. "Never forget him."

"Oh, I wouldn't dare," Stella replied with a grin. "Even when he scowls like thunderclouds."

As Stella left the study, Margot remained by the fire, her mind running over the events of the day. Something was missing. A piece of the puzzle. She could feel it.

Somewhere in the halls of Blackwell Manor, someone was growing desperate. And desperate people made mistakes.

And when they did, Margot would be watching.

argot leaned back in her oak chair within her study, recent events tangled in her thoughts like the creeping roses on the manor's grand trellis. She had barely taken a sip of her tea when Stella burst in—her expression gleaming with both anticipation and curiosity, tempered by her usual wit.

"There's a villager downstairs—says he's found something of interest," Stella announced with characteristic flair.

Margot arched an eyebrow. "Well, I suppose I could use a dose of Crayford intrigue over my tea. Show him in."

Moments later, Billy, the delivery boy turned general purveyor of local gossip, shuffled into the study, hat in hand. Behind him stood Mr Abbey, a local fisherman who often turned up with reports of slippery trout and slipperier rumours.

"Lady Blackwell," Abbey began, bobbing his head in exaggerated reverence. "I reckon I saw someone early this morning, down by the river."

Margot regarded him with polite patience. "The river at dawn? You seem to have a sharp eye for the peculiar in such faint light, Mr Abbey."

Abbey twisted his cap nervously. "I'm certain of what I saw, ma'am. It was that composer fellow—Mr Lambrook. He was standing by the water, looking... well, not himself, if you catch my meaning. Shifty-like."

Margot's brow furrowed. "Shifty, Mr Abbey? That's quite an accusation for a fleeting glance."

"That composer wears fine boots, don't he?" Abbey countered. "Covered in mud this morning, they were. River mud—you'd know it anywhere."

A ripple of suspicion crossed Margot's face. "Thank you, Mr Abbey. This is most interesting. Stella, see our guests out, and inform Inspector Grant that I should like a word."

When Simon Grant appeared not long after, he brought both his predilection for doubt and a keen readiness to cross-examine.

"River mud," Simon began, pacing. "If that's true, it places Augustus in the very sort of inconvenient position he's grown accustomed to."

"Indeed," Margot replied, her voice carrying the weight of thought. "It's worth considering whether Mr Abbey's observations were tinged with embellishment or whether they unveil yet another piece to our puzzle."

"Only one way to know," Simon said briskly, setting down his hat and motioning for his notebook. "Let's see to Lambrook and his boots."

. . .

Margot and Simon found Augustus in the conservatory, hunched over a piano, tapped keys spilling quiet, mournful notes into the air. As the pair entered, Augustus glanced back, his always-pensive countenance registering unease.

"Inspector," he greeted Simon, though his voice faltered. "Lady Blackwell."

"Mr Lambrook," Simon said curtly, his boots clicking as he closed the distance. "You wouldn't happen to have been by the river this morning, would you?"

"The river?" Augustus echoed, his fingers hovering above the keys. "I... walked for air, as I often do. But I didn't linger near the water."

"We have a fisherman's word tying you there," Margot offered, her tone light but probing. "And your unusually muddy boots seem to corroborate his claim."

Augustus exhaled sharply, standing now, his jaw tight. "It's not a crime to walk by the water. Besides, why would I go there at dawn of all times?"

"Perhaps to discard something?" Simon suggested pointedly, his voice carrying an edge to it.

"To discard—? No!" Augustus snapped, his frustration spilling out. "I don't know why my boots are cause for such scrutiny."

Simon leaned in closer, his features unmistakably sceptical. "But you do admit they're muddy."

"I won't deny that," Augustus conceded grudgingly. "But can we stop pretending that mud makes me a murderer?"

Margot's sharp eyes met Simon's before flicking back to Augustus. "Mud, perhaps not. But deception might."

———

When the matter of Augustus's boots shifted to the background, another peculiar detail caught Margot's keen observation: Irene Castell's shoes. She had spotted the young woman earlier in the parlour, her hemline conspicuously dirtied, her shoes caked with dried mud. This went unnoticed until Margot addressed her directly later that afternoon.

"Irene," Margot began as they crossed paths near the drawing room. "You appear to have been battling some rather messy terrain. Might I ask what possessed you to brave the mud in such fine footwear?"

Irene froze, her face flushing. "It… it rained briefly when I was outside," she stammered.

Margot arched a sceptical brow. "And why, pray, were you outside at such an odd hour?"

"I was fetching water," Irene blurted. "The jugs for Madame Celeste's flower displays needed refilling."

"By the river?" Simon, who had approached from the hallway, interjected with his signature scepticism. He crossed his arms, watching her intently.

"Well, directly from the outer garden," Irene corrected hurriedly, though her cheeks burned. "It was muddy… I didn't think it mattered."

"Convenient," Simon muttered.

"And yet highly questionable," Margot added, though her voice remained cool. "Perhaps a detail I should follow up with Mrs Henshaw."

Irene, clearly flustered, mumbled an excuse and quickly excused herself. But the mud on both Augustus and Irene's shoes added yet another ripple of confusion to an already murky narrative.

———

As night fell, Madame Celeste joined Margot for tea in the drawing room, her usually pristine composure somewhat dulled by her use of laudanum. The opium tincture seemed to paint her movements with an air of detachment, her hands slower than usual as she lifted her cup to her lips.

"I grow tired of this dreariness," Celeste murmured, her voice heavy with weariness. "It weighs on me more with each passing day."

Margot sipped her tea, watching her guest closely. "I imagine the melancholy of unanswered questions hardly helps."

"Oh, the questions," Celeste sighed theatrically, reaching for a biscuit but abandoning the attempt midway. "Sometimes I feel as though I'm living through dreams rather than days."

There was a pause, and then Celeste's brow furrowed faintly. "Last night," she began haltingly, "I was here—I mean, not here but... somewhere else in the house. I remember crying. Someone comforted me... a man, I think, but I can't recall who."

Margot set her tea down carefully. "Someone comforted you?" she repeated, her voice carefully neutral. "Do you remember what was said?"

"It was whispered... and kind." Celeste's expression softened briefly before tightening again. "But... it might've been a dream, for all I know."

Simon, who entered with barely a knock, caught the end of the exchange. "Dreams and timelines," he said flatly. "In this house, both seem equally unreliable."

Margot glanced at him, her expression contemplative. "Perhaps," she agreed. "But even unreliable fragments can lead to the truth."

Simon didn't reply, though his thoughtful silence carried its own weight of agreement.

————

Back in her study that evening, Margot sat staring at her notes, each detail recorded in precise handwriting. River mud, muddied shoes, laudanum-induced whispers—all scattered pieces of a puzzle still refusing to fit together. Behind her, Stella interrupted her thoughts as she entered with the evening's post.

"I'll say this," Stella remarked as she placed the letters on the desk. "Blackwell Manor has no shortage of mysteries or suspects. If solving one murder is this much work, thank heavens there hasn't been a second."

Margot, for once, chuckled softly. "Indeed, Stella. One bout of murder is quite enough for a lifetime."

As Stella slipped away, Margot's eyes returned to her notes, her mind sharp and ready to untangle the truth. Somewhere amidst the mud, the whispers, and the ever-present shadows of Blackwell Manor, lay the answer she sought and she was more determined than ever to find it.

22

The west garden at Blackwell Manor, a lush expanse of winding hedgerows and vivid blossoms, served as a small refuge for Margot in troublesome times. But today, as she moved idly along its gravel paths, her mind hummed with speculation over the twists of Evelyn Linwood's murder. The once-innocuous details, the misplaced items, the suspicious timing—they all threaded into a tapestry too knotted to make sense of yet.

It was as she passed a gutter near the garden wall that a glint of light caught her eye—a thin, silver gleam that sparked an instinctive pause. Crouching, she withdrew a handkerchief from her pocket and carefully pried free an ornate hairpin from the metal grate. Intricate engravings curled across its surface, and Margot suddenly recalled seeing the very same hairpin on Evelyn just days before her life was so mercilessly cut short.

Margot turned the pin over in her hands, pondering its significance. "Celeste lent it to her," she murmured to herself.

"But why has it managed to find its way into a gutter, far from either Evelyn or Celeste's rooms?"

The memory of Irene Castell's frequent presence in Celeste's dressing room flitted across her mind. Irene had access to Celeste's belongings, as did Augustus Lambrook, given his consultations about their rehearsals. But accessing the dressing room wasn't proof—yet the delicate and deliberate artistry of the pin suggested this clue was far from accidental.

Returning to the parlour with the hairpin carefully wrapped in a handkerchief, Margot found Simon Grant sitting stiffly, his usually composed demeanour strained under the weight of their increasingly convoluted investigation. Papers were strewn about the small table between them, each scribbled with interviews, timelines, and theories—but nothing seemed to connect the central lines of intrigue.

"Let me guess," Simon said as she placed the pin on the table before him. "A bauble rediscovered in a Cinderella-esque twist?"

"Hardly." Margot sat opposite him, her gaze unwavering. "I found this outside, near the gutter just by the west garden wall. Evelyn borrowed it from Celeste shortly before her passing. I'd wager it carries more bearing to her story than one might first assume."

Simon took the pin in hand, turning it to catch the glint of light. "Irene and Augustus had countless reasons to be near Celeste's room," he mused. "Though Celeste, of course, would sooner turn these discoveries into melodrama than clear answers."

"And Jacques remains a looming presence, doesn't he?" Margot added lightly. "He strikes me as one unafraid to pocket or plant intriguing pieces. One never knows when they might prove useful."

Simon exhaled sharply. "Every clue seems crafted to deepen the mire." He sat back heavily. "But this—these timelines and trinkets—it's shifting dangerously. My superiors are breathing down my neck, demanding swift resolution." He ran a hand briskly through his hair. "At this rate, I'll be returning their inquiries not with suspects but with a sprawling net of impossibilities."

Margot leaned forward slightly. "I do sympathise with your plight, Inspector. But like the best recitals, the grand conclusion only strikes when every secret note aligns."

———

The hum of Blackwell Manor's staff was both a comfort and a distraction as Margot made her way through the kitchens. Her mind lingered on Irene Castell, whose explanations and alibis—though seemingly plausible—blended into a mesh of half-believable narratives that felt more like a carefully rehearsed play than the truth. Margot's sharpened instinct told her there was no smoke without fire.

Margot found Mrs Henshaw presiding over the kitchen like an admiral among her fleet, supervising the preparation of scones for the morning tea tray. Irene had allegedly been seen here during part of the other day's chaos. It was time to confirm how much truth lived in this.

"Mrs Henshaw, it seems Irene had been quite industrious during the other day's... disturbances," Margot began. "I hear she was here in the kitchens when Tom made rather a spectacle over missing silver napkin rings."

The housekeeper paused for the briefest of moments, her expression impassive. "She was here, milady," Mrs Henshaw replied. "Mending a hem on one of Madame Celeste's evening gowns and making sure we had enough chamomile tea for her," Mrs Henshaw said briskly. "She left shortly before the ruckus erupted."

"Naturally," Margot murmured, filing Mrs Henshaw's testimony in the ever-growing mental ledger of Irene's whereabouts.

Satisfied with this line of questioning, Margot moved next to the parlour, where she found Betsy, the young maid known for her bright chatter when the mood struck. Betsy looked up from her dusting, startled to see Lady Blackwell sweep into the room.

"Betsy," Margot began, her tone light, "I require your assistance on a small matter. Irene Castell—do you recall her stepping in to mediate between Tom and Mary during their spat?"

"Oh yes, milady," Betsy replied eagerly. "She was quite firm with them, though I think she favoured Mary a bit. Poor Tom didn't take it well."

"And where was this?" Margot pressed.

"In the scullery," Betsy answered promptly. "They were loud enough for the whole hall to hear."

Margot gave a faint smile. "Thank you, Betsy. That will be all."

As she left the parlour, Margot's brows furrowed slightly. Each thread provided by the staff was consistent— irritatingly consistent. Irene was either managing to barely stay ahead of suspicion or was simply so innocuous her presence was entirely benign.

This maddening consistency carried on into the gardens, where Margot stumbled across Stella in deep conversation with Tom himself. Upon spotting Margot, Stella gave an exaggerated sigh and muttered, "He'll make a fine novelist if this keeps up, won't he, milady?"

Margot turned to Tom, fixing him with a piercing gaze. "And what story are we spinning now, Tom?"

Tom flushed, twisting his cap nervously. "It's just about Irene, milady. She's always... fluttering about, see? Never settles in one place long. Always here to help but also... there."

"She gave you an earful about the napkin rings, I take it?" Margot asked drily.

Tom huffed. "She did, though Mary got off lighter than I did. Only meant to say she's quick at popping up when there's trouble."

Margot tilted her head, the wheels turning in her mind. "Curious," she murmured, "how ubiquitous she seems to be."

By the time Margot returned indoors, her patience for Irene's perfectly placed alibis was thinning rapidly. Too many wheels seemed to turn too neatly in Irene Castell's favour— and Margot suspected she wasn't the only one beginning to feel the sharp edge of frustration.

Someone at Blackwell Manor was a killer. That much was certain. And if the whispers and uneasy glances were anything to go by, the murderer was still among the guests.

Margot felt as though she were caught in an elegant trap. One spun from polished lies and practiced innocence. Every smile concealed a motive, every alibi held just enough truth to raise doubt. Still, she clung to one thing: the belief that the truth, no matter how deeply buried, would surface.

But what if it didn't? What if this was the one mystery she could not untangle—one that would stain the halls of Blackwell Manor forever?

She shook off the chill creeping up her spine. No. She would not let Blackwell become a house of unanswered questions. Not while she still had breath and wit.

---

23

*T*he dining room at Blackwell Manor shimmered beneath the freshly repaired chandelier, its crystals casting refracted light that danced across the ceiling like little spectres. The long mahogany table was laid with Margot's finest china and gleaming silverware, the place settings so meticulously arranged they seemed to defy the growing undercurrent of discord.

It was in every superficial sense a dinner of elegance and grace. And yet, beneath the polished surface, the true purpose simmered—this was no social gathering, but a calculated arrangement, and Margot its architect. She sat at the head of the table, posture regal, her expression composed, though her eyes flicked from guest to guest with the same discerning scrutiny one might reserve for cards in a high-stakes game of whist.

To her left sat Jacques Maroni, his air of polished detachment intact, though Margot didn't miss the way his eyes scanned the room—nervous, predatory, calculating. Augustus Lambrook occupied the seat directly across from him, cheeks flushed with either indignation or sherry—it was difficult to tell which. Further down the table, beside Madame Celeste, was Irene Castell, her pale hands twitching slightly as she adjusted her napkin for the fourth time in as many minutes. Though her smile remained politely pinned in place, it trembled at the edges like parchment too close to flame.

Margot allowed the conversation to flow freely for a time. It was Jacques, predictably, who held court, his voice slick with self-assurance as he regaled the table with tales of theatrical triumphs and backstage chaos.

"It's a balancing act," Jacques said, raising his wine glass with an easy flourish. "Managing egos, temperaments, finances… and of course, the occasional petty grievance."

Across the table, Augustus stiffened. "Petty?" he echoed. "Is that what you're calling them now?"

Jacques offered a lazy smile, though his eyes narrowed. "Well, one learns to put such things into perspective."

Margot spoke, her tone smooth but cool. "And yet, one might argue that ignoring grievances only allows them to fester into something altogether less petty."

Jacques turned toward her with a look of amusement that didn't quite reach his eyes. "Lady Blackwell, you always did have a gift for seeing the rot beneath the roses."

"I simply prefer my roses without thorns, Monsieur Maroni," she replied, lifting her glass in a mock toast.

It was only a matter of time before the pleasantries began to unravel. Margot intended it that way. She'd long learned that the illusion of comfort often loosened tongues far more effectively than interrogation ever could.

Soon, the conversation drifted, by no accident of chance, toward Evelyn's untimely death.

"She was always interfering," Jacques said, more sharply now. "Couldn't let anything progress without her hand stirring the pot."

"Or perhaps," Augustus cut in, his tone brittle, "she simply couldn't abide mediocrity."

Jacques's smirk curled, his jaw tightening like a vice. "Ever the gentleman, Augustus," he sneered. "Though I daresay it takes real talent to find grace in a woman who mistook shrieking for soprano and drama for depth. But then, Evelyn always did fancy herself a diva—stage lights or not."

Margot leaned forward slightly, keeping her voice low but firm. "And yet it seems none of you recall Evelyn with anything resembling fondness."

Augustus looked away, muttering, "She had her moments."

"Yes," Margot said softly, "but the kind of moments that seem to linger like the scent of laudanum—heady, bitter, and hard to forget."

A silence fell across the table, broken only by the clink of cutlery and the faint murmur of the fire. Irene, seated uncomfortably close to the rising heat of tension, suddenly snapped.

"I don't see what this achieves," she said, her voice trembling. "Evelyn's dead, and yet here we are, clawing at one another like carrion birds."

Jacques turned to her, lips curling into something between amusement and menace. "Perhaps that's because some of us are more feathered than others."

"Enough," Celeste interjected, her voice steadier than it had been in days. "This bickering does nothing but dishonour her memory."

"Her memory?" Augustus scoffed. "Forgive me, Madame, but Evelyn inspired many things. Loyalty was not one of them."

"And yet," Jacques muttered, "she had no shortage of people willing to pretend otherwise."

Margot turned her attention to Irene. The girl sat with her head down, staring at the untouched food on her plate. Her knuckles had gone white where she gripped her napkin. Now seemed to be the moment.

"Irene," Margot said gently, "you spent more time with Evelyn than most. You were trusted. Perhaps you noticed something, anything, that might help us understand her state of mind before her death?"

Irene looked up sharply, eyes wide and glassy. "I... I don't know. She was difficult, yes, but that's hardly a motive for—"

"I'm not accusing you, my dear," Margot said. "But those who are difficult often suffer quietly. Was Evelyn afraid? Agitated? Did she speak of threats?"

"I—no. Maybe. I'm sorry, I need some air." Without waiting for permission or excuse, Irene pushed back her chair and fled the room, footsteps echoing through the corridor.

Margot watched her go, her mind working furiously.

———

By the time dessert was served—a delicate lemon syllabub that no one touched—the room had fallen into a brittle, uneasy quiet. Simon Grant, who had remained largely silent during the meal, sat with arms folded and brow furrowed. He cast Margot a look she recognised: the barely concealed tension of a man burdened by too many expectations and too few answers.

At last, he spoke. "There is one detail we've yet to confront directly," he said, his voice low and grave. "The gloves. The ones found in Madame Celeste's quarters."

Celeste, who had thus far remained aloof, met his gaze squarely. "Gloves are hardly unusual in a house of this size."

Simon nodded slowly. "True. But gloves with traces of metallic residue and fragments of theatre paint are less common. And their movement—from one part of the house to another—suggests they were either planted, or carried by someone who wanted them forgotten."

Jacques raised an eyebrow. "And what exactly are you implying, Inspector?"

"That someone at this table knows how they came to be where they were."

Silence again. Even the chandelier's soft jingling seemed to quiet, as though the room itself held its breath.

Margot looked to the empty seat beside Celeste. "It's always interesting, isn't it, how people and objects migrate—how they end up in the wrong places, and yet seem so right for misdirection."

Stella, perched quietly in the corner, leaned in and whispered, "They couldn't make themselves look guiltier if they wore signboards."

Margot didn't smile this time. Her mind was racing—across gardens and dressing rooms, through arguments and alliances, along corridors both literal and metaphorical. The gloves, the shattered chandelier, the burnt letters, the silences, the glances—it all spiralled inward toward something vital.

She looked once more at her guests—Jacques, theatrical and defensive; Augustus, bitter and unravelling; Celeste, proud and enigmatic. And Irene, missing.

"We're getting close," she murmured to Simon, who nodded grimly.

"Let's just hope," he said under his breath, "we get there before someone else ends up dead."

24

*T*he morning after the uneasy dinner, Blackwell Manor held its breath.

Gone was the familiar rhythm of domesticity: the faint clatter of dishes from the kitchens, the soft rustle of skirts along the corridors, the occasional burst of laughter from the maids. In their place was a hush so profound it seemed the very walls were listening. Margot stood in the library, eyes scanning the same page of a book she'd not turned for twenty minutes, her thoughts too loud to let any words sink in.

She had slept little, her mind turning restlessly through what she knew—and what she still didn't. Evelyn Linwood's death had cast a long shadow, and in its wake lay a trail of secrets yet untangled. Margot set the book aside and moved to the window, watching the mist cling to the gardens like a silken veil.

Madame Celeste... Irene Castell... Augustus Lambrook... Jacques

Maroni... Evelyn's threats... the borrowed composition... burnt letters...

Her gaze drifted, unfocused, until it settled on the grand piano in the music room across the hall. A sudden memory flared—Evelyn at the piano, snipping a length of wire to repair her sheet music folder. That same fine, metallic thread. Unusual, not something most carried. Unless...

Margot turned sharply.

Her footsteps were swift but silent as she made her way upstairs, skirts whispering over the polished floorboards. Irene Castell's room was modest, tidy, as befitted a companion and aspiring musician. The sunlight barely reached inside, leaving the room in a soft gloom. A small sewing kit rested on the dressing table, lid closed, innocent enough.

Margot hesitated only briefly before opening it.

Neatly folded threads, a few pins, buttons. And then, tucked beneath the false bottom, a roll of fine piano wire.

She stared at it, her heart tightening. The gauge, the sheen—identical to the piece Simon had shown her days ago. It had been easy to dismiss Evelyn's string as common enough. But this? Hidden away?

Margot's jaw tightened as the pieces clicked into place with unnerving clarity.

She didn't wait. Within moments, she was striding down the corridor, wire wrapped carefully in her handkerchief.

———

Inspector Simon Grant looked up from his papers as she entered the dining room, her eyes lit with quiet fire.

"I think I've found something," she said without preamble, extending the cloth-wrapped bundle.

Simon unfolded it slowly, his brow furrowing as he revealed the piano wire.

"Where did you—?"

"In Irene's sewing kit," Margot said crisply. "Hidden beneath a false bottom. Not the sort of item one misplaces by accident."

Simon's jaw tensed as he held the wire between his fingers, examining it with the detached eye of experience. "Same type, no doubt. Just like the one used on Evelyn."

Margot folded her arms slowly, her voice low and laced with quiet intensity. "Irene was Madame Celeste's shadow—always near, always watching. If this wire is what I believe it is... then Irene isn't just implicated. She's at the heart of Evelyn's murder."

Simon let out a slow breath. "We need to speak to her. Now."

———

They found Irene Castell seated in the drawing room, staring blankly out the window at the fading mist. Her hands were folded in her lap, the very picture of calm—until she turned and saw them.

Margot didn't sit. She stood, poised yet unrelenting, the roll of wire now resting plainly in her gloved hand.

"Irene," she said softly, "we need to speak with you."

169

The young woman blinked, then nodded slowly. "Of course."

Simon closed the door behind them. "We found this in your belongings," he said without ceremony, placing the wire on the table before her. "Care to explain how it came to be in your sewing kit?"

Irene's eyes widened, flicking to the wire and back again. Her hands clenched unconsciously.

"That's not mine," she said quickly. "I don't—someone must have planted it."

Margot's voice remained gentle. "It was beneath a false bottom. In your personal sewing kit. That's not something one stumbles upon accidentally, Irene."

"I don't know how it got there," Irene insisted. "I swear it."

Simon stepped forward. "This is the same wire that killed Evelyn Linwood. Your presence in the house, your connection to Madame Celeste, and now this—don't make this harder than it already is."

Irene opened her mouth, closed it again. Her shoulders began to shake.

"I… I didn't mean to…" she whispered. "It wasn't supposed to happen like that."

Margot remained still, letting the words settle. "Tell us what did happen."

Irene sank into a chair, her face crumpling as tears welled in her eyes. "She was going to ruin her. Evelyn… she said she had proof. Letters, drafts—showing that Madame Celeste had lifted sections from a colleague's composition and passed them off as her own. She was going to publish it. Destroy everything."

Margot sat down at last, her tone calm but firm. "So you confronted her?"

"I wanted to plead with her," Irene said, voice trembling. "To ask her to reconsider. Madame Celeste has worked her whole life—her career, her reputation, it would all be gone."

"What happened in that room?" Simon asked.

Irene looked away. "She laughed at me. Said Madame deserved it. Said she was a fraud, and that the world should know it. I was so angry. I tried to reason with her, but she kept taunting me. And then I saw the wire. It was just sitting there..."

There was a long silence.

"I didn't plan to kill her," Irene whispered, her voice breaking. "But I... I just couldn't let her destroy Madame Celeste."

"Tell us exactly what happened that night," Simon said, his voice firm but not unkind.

Irene took a shuddering breath. "I overheard Evelyn on the telephone. She was speaking to a music critic from London —describing how she had proof that would ruin Madame Celeste forever. She said she'd been waiting years for this moment."

"And that's when you confronted her?" Margot asked.

"Not immediately," Irene said, twisting her handkerchief. "I waited until evening, when I knew she'd be alone in the music room. I begged her to reconsider, reminded her how many lives would be affected. She laughed at me—called me pathetic, said I was nothing but a failed pianist living vicariously through Celeste's fading glory."

Her voice hardened. "She said Celeste had been deceiving audiences for years, and that it was time everyone knew the truth. That's when I saw the wire... It was just sitting there on the piano. She used it to bind her sheet music."

Irene's eyes filled with tears. "I picked it up without thinking. Just wanted to frighten her, to make her stop talking. But she kept taunting me, saying I was nothing, would always be nothing. And then... and then my hands were around the wire, and it was around her neck, and everything happened so fast..."

She collapsed into sobs. "When she fell, I panicked. I ran. I hid the gloves I'd been wearing. I tried to act normal. But every night since then, I hear her voice. Every night, I feel the wire in my hands."

"And the 'outsider' Evelyn mentioned in her diary?" Simon pressed.

Irene looked down. "That was me. She called me that—said I was an outsider pretending to belong in Madame Celeste's world. She wrote about me that way to mock my ambitions."

"You were seen," Simon said quietly. "By the delivery boy, Billy. He noticed your limp." Irene's eyes widened. "I... I twisted my ankle fleeing the scene. I didn't realise anyone had seen me. I've been terrified ever since, waiting for someone to mention it."

She buried her face in her hands.

Margot's heart ached, though her expression remained composed. "You tried to protect someone you admired. But in doing so, you destroyed another life and your own."

"I know," Irene sobbed. "I know."

By mid-afternoon, the constables had arrived. Irene Castell didn't protest as she was led through the halls of Blackwell Manor. Her head remained bowed, her steps slow. The household staff watched from doorways and corridors, murmuring in subdued tones.

Margot stood in the foyer, hands clasped before her, eyes following the young woman until the police car doors shut with a dull thud.

"She was barely more than a girl," Margot said softly.

Simon stood beside her. "She made a terrible choice. But not out of cruelty."

"No," Margot agreed, "out of misplaced loyalty and fear."

They watched the police car disappear into the mist. The fog was lifting now, revealing the bare outlines of the rose garden in the distance.

"How many lives has this ruined?" Margot asked, mostly to herself.

Simon didn't answer. The question lingered.

Later, Margot returned to the music room. The piano sat silently, its keys untouched, its lid half-open as though waiting for someone to return.

She looked down at the bench where Evelyn once sat, then to the windowsill where Irene had lingered, always on the periphery of things.

Everything had changed.

Evelyn Linwood was gone. Irene Castell was in custody. Madame Celeste's career, though protected for now, was built on a fragile lie. And Margot herself felt changed, too. A layer of innocence had been peeled back from Blackwell Manor, revealing the darker threads that bound even the most refined among them.

She touched the edge of the piano, then turned away.

The case was closed, but the echo of Evelyn's final notes would linger.

25

The morning after Irene Castell's dramatic confession and arrest carried a heavy silence through Blackwell Manor, broken only by the occasional rustle of footsteps on polished floors as the household attempted to resume its daily rhythms. Margot, ever the pillar of composure, sat at her writing desk contemplating the wreckage that Evelyn's murder, and its fallout, had wrought upon the manor's once-dignified halls.

She was interrupted by the brisk entrance of Jacques Maroni, unmistakable in his finely tailored travelling coat and with his ever-present air of calculated detachment. But something about Jacques was different today: the gleam in his eye lacked its usual cockiness, and his steps, though polished, betrayed a faint tremor.

"Lady Blackwell," Jacques said tersely, placing his gloves on the edge of her desk. "I'll not trouble you much longer. I've come to bid you farewell."

Margot arched an elegant brow. "Leaving us so soon, Jacques?"

"A telegram arrived this morning," he said, his voice strained. "My financial... irregularities have been discovered by the Opera Board. They're launching a formal investigation. I'm to report to London immediately." He attempted his usual charm but failed. "It seems Evelyn's accusations have found their mark, even from beyond the grave."

As he adjusted the brim of his hat and swept toward the door, Stella Wickham appeared in the hall, leaning casually against the balustrade. "Between the fraud, the murder, and the drama," she remarked with a smirk, "this place might need an exorcist."

Jacques paused for the briefest of moments before continuing on his way, his exit marked by the echo of hastily packed trunks being loaded into a waiting car. Margot watched him go, her expression inscrutable but her thoughts churning. Jacques Maroni was a man adept at orchestrating scandals, but as the dust settled, it became clear that even his charms had their limits.

———

Later in the afternoon, Augustus Lambrook sought Margot out in the conservatory, where the sunlight dappled the floor in shifting patterns as clouds skittered across the sky. Augustus looked as if he hadn't slept, his usually melancholy expression deepened by shadows under his eyes. In his hand, he clutched a small, battered notebook, which he turned over nervously as he approached.

"Lady Blackwell," Augustus began, his voice soft but earnest. "I owe you... I owe you an apology."

Margot gestured for him to sit, though her expression suggested she expected far more than an apology. "Go on, Mr Lambrook."

Augustus hesitated, his fingers running over the leather cover of the notebook. "I… I should have spoken up earlier. About everything. The threats, her hold over me… God, I was such a coward. She knew exactly where to press, which weaknesses to exploit."

"You feared that her revelations about your past would ruin you," Margot said plainly, her gaze unwavering. "And so you remained silent."

Augustus nodded miserably. "She had evidence—proof of my… indiscretions. I thought if I kept my head down, if I stayed out of her way, she'd move on. But she never did. And now…"

He trailed off, his voice thick with regret. "Sometimes the truth takes more courage than I have."

Margot studied him for a long moment before finally speaking. "Perhaps, Augustus, it's not too late for a fresh start. But running from the truth does not constitute courage —it merely delays the consequences."

Augustus looked up at her, his eyes filled with a mixture of gratitude and shame. "You're right, of course. Thank you, Lady Blackwell. For your kindness… and your candour."

As he rose to leave, Stella intercepted Margot with her characteristic wit. "He looks like a thunderstorm walking," she remarked drily, "but maybe he'll find his sun somewhere else."

Margot allowed herself a faint smile, though her thoughts were heavy. Augustus Lambrook, burdened by his guilt and shadowed by his choices, was one of many casualties in a tragedy that had spared no one.

———

The day's final encounter came shortly before sunset, when Margot visited Madame Celeste in her private quarters. The once-grand opera singer was a shadow of her former self, her figure slouched as she folded the last of her belongings into a trunk. Her eyes, rimmed with red, carried a weariness that no amount of powder or rouge could conceal.

"Lady Blackwell," Celeste murmured, her voice barely above a whisper. "You honour me with your visit. Though I imagine you've little patience left for my theatrics."

Margot approached the vanity, where a half-packed collection of jewels and perfumes lay scattered. "I came to see if you required anything before your departure, Madame," she said gently. "It seems Blackwell Manor has been... unkind to you."

Celeste let out a choked laugh, though tears glistened in her eyes. "Blackwell Manor has been the stage where my life unravelled," she breathed, her hands trembling as she closed the lid of her jewellery box. "Evelyn knew the truth about my voice—that it wasn't merely lost, but ruined by years of pushing beyond my natural range. She threatened to expose how I'd been lip-syncing at private performances, using recordings from my prime years. The shame of that revelation would have destroyed what little remained of my career. Irene knew too; she helped orchestrate the deception, believing she was protecting me."

Margot clasped her hands, stricken by the sight of a woman undone.

Celeste looked at her then, her eyes swimming with emotion. "I no longer belong in the limelight, Lady Blackwell. My voice is gone, my reputation in tatters. I no longer wish to remain in the public eye."

There was a long pause before Celeste added, "But I will always remember your kindness, Margot. You gave me refuge when I had nowhere else to turn."

Margot inclined her head gracefully. "And perhaps you'll find refuge elsewhere, away from the shadows of the stage."

Celeste nodded, her tears spilling over as she turned back to her trunk. As Margot left the room, the weight of the day's farewells pressed upon her. Blackwell Manor, though still standing proud, had been forever changed by the events of Evelyn Linwood's murder. And as the sun dipped below the horizon, casting the estate in a long shadow, Margot couldn't help but wonder what new dawns or storms lay ahead.

he morning sun cast a golden glow over Blackwell Manor, its light dancing through the tall, symmetrical windows and pooling across the gleaming floorboards of the dining room. Margot sat at the head of the long mahogany table, her morning tea momentarily forgotten as she held a letter between her fingers. Her brow quirked with wry amusement as she read the precise, clipped handwriting of Inspector Simon Grant.

"I hope this finds you planning fewer dinner parties with murderers this season," the note read.

Margot allowed herself a soft chuckle, folding the paper with a neat snap before placing it beside her saucer. Stella Wickham, her ever-watchful lady's maid and confidante, appeared in the doorway holding a fresh tray of letters. Her sharp eyes immediately caught the twinkle in Margot's gaze.

"Let me guess," Stella said, her voice laced with dry amusement, "Inspector Dour has sent another one of his charming morning insults?"

"Right on cue," Margot replied, gesturing toward the letter. "He does have a talent for subtle barbs."

Stella took the note and skimmed it, her lips curling into a smirk. "A little harsh, but not wholly undeserved. You have to admit, the guest list for your last dinner did rather take a turn."

Margot rose from her chair, gathering her dressing gown more closely around her as she looked out at the mist-softened view of the gardens. "Blackwell Manor has always attracted a certain level of drama. But I must say, even I hadn't expected our last soiree to end in suspicion and scandal."

"If we keep this up," Stella said, setting down the tray, "we'll need to hire a full-time constable for the west wing."

Margot laughed lightly. "Oh, let's not give Simon ideas."

———

Later that day, with the air crisp and alive with the scent of freshly turned soil, Margot took a leisurely walk through the village. Though recent weeks had brought shadows to Crayford, she was determined to tilt the town back toward warmth. Her thoughts turned to the upcoming season—what the village needed, she decided, was an event. Something light-hearted. Something joyful.

By the time she returned to the manor, her mind was set.

"We'll hold a village-wide singing contest," she announced to Stella, who looked up from her embroidery with one arched brow.

"You plan to make the villagers sing for their sanity?"

"No," Margot said, breezing past her, "I plan to make them sing for their spirits. There's been too much silence lately— the wrong kind."

With Stella trailing behind and already questioning the logistics, Margot sat down to draft the announcement. Her handwriting, fluid and elegant, danced across the page with phrases like *'celebration of voice,'* and *'a festival of joy.'* She envisioned laughter on the manor lawns, bunting strung from tree to tree, and Crayford's best (and perhaps worst) singers given their moment in the sun.

The next day, Margot ventured into town to gather support. Her first stop was the bakery, where Mrs Tillyrose bustled about with sugar-dusted elbows and a tray of steaming jam tarts.

"A singing competition?" the baker exclaimed, eyes lighting up. "Oh, Lady Margot, that's just the thing! Remind the town that we're still a place for joy."

"That's precisely the idea," Margot replied, accepting a tart with a grateful smile. "Will you enter?"

Mrs Tillyrose laughed, waving a floured hand. "Only if the judging's based on volume rather than pitch."

As Margot stepped outside, she was nearly bowled over by young Billy, the delivery boy, who skidded to a halt with a bundle of newspapers under his arm.

"Heard you're organising a singing thing," he panted, eyes bright. "Think I could try out? I mean, I can't hold a note for long, but I've got enthusiasm."

Before Margot could reply, Stella, who had followed a few steps behind, interjected with a smirk. "Enthusiasm may be your only asset, Billy, but that's half the battle."

Billy grinned. "Then I'm halfway to stardom!"

Margot, amused, gave the boy an encouraging nod. "That's the spirit."

Back at the manor, preparations began in earnest. Stella oversaw the placement of chairs and bunting with military precision, directing footmen like chess pieces. "I want symmetry, not chaos," she declared. "And do mind the grass. Lady Margot would prefer not to host a contest in a muddy trench."

Margot, meanwhile, sat at her writing desk composing a letter addressed in careful script: *To Madame Celeste, London.*

Her note struck a tone of gentle invitation and admiration. "The people of Crayford could benefit from your eye and your ear," she wrote. "Might you consider serving as a guest judge for our village singing contest?"

The envelope was sealed with the Blackwell crest and sent the very next morning.

———

Days passed, and excitement buzzed like bees over lavender. Posters appeared in the town square. Choirs practiced in church halls. Children sang off-key in the streets. The manor grounds transformed into a stage, with rows of white chairs and flower-laced bunting strung between yew trees.

On the morning of the contest, the manor hummed with activity. Footmen carried lemonade and sponge cake to tables, while Stella did a final inspection, clipboard in hand.

And then, just as the first notes of the contest were about to ring out, the sound of a powerful engine turned every head.

A silver Rolls-Royce glided down the drive.

Gasps rippled through the crowd as it came to a slow, regal stop. The driver, dressed in black with a cap perched properly, stepped out to open the passenger door.

Madame Celeste emerged like a queen from a fairy tale—elegant, poised, and unmissable. Gone were the theatrical gowns of her stage days. In their place, she wore a refined navy ensemble with a brooch shaped like a treble clef.

The villagers whispered excitedly. Someone dropped a scone.

Margot approached with a delighted smile. "You made it."

Celeste's eyes sparkled. "I never could resist a good aria—even if it's sung by sheep farmers."

Margot laughed softly. "Welcome to Crayford's most melodious gathering."

Celeste took her place at the judging table beside Reverend Blithe and Mrs Tillyrose, who was fanning herself furiously. Children lined up with bright ribbons in their hair, and grown men cleared their throats like nervous schoolboys.

As the first contestant, a nervous farmhand with a lovely baritone, took the stage, Margot stepped to the side of the lawn. She scanned the crowd—laughter, song, even the occasional off-key warble filled the spring air. Blackwell Manor once again pulsed with life.

Beside her, Stella folded her arms and nodded in satisfaction. "Well, Lady Margot, you've done it again. A peaceful event without a single corpse."

Margot smiled. "Let's not tempt fate. It's only intermission."

But even as she said it, a deeper calm settled within her. Perhaps, at long last, the music would carry them into a gentler season.

$\mathcal{T}$he grounds of Blackwell Manor shimmered under the subtle glow of twilight, lanterns softly illuminating the garden as Margot leaned against the balustrade of the terrace. The air was balmy, carrying the scent of roses and the faint echoes of earlier laughter from the singing contest that had taken place that afternoon. For the first time in what felt like ages, the manor was alive not with suspicion or secrets, but with joy, song, and the camaraderie of a community brought together.

Margot took a deep breath, letting the peace of the moment settle over her. The singing contest had exceeded all expectations. Villagers of all ages had gathered on the lawn, their voices mingling in shared celebration. Even young Billy, the spirited delivery boy, had surprised everyone with a sweet, if slightly off-key, rendition of a popular folk song that had prompted a warm round of applause. And Madame Celeste, sitting quietly among the judges, had offered soft words of encouragement to each participant, her presence a quiet grace that even Mrs Tillyrose, the meddlesome baker, had to admire.

Stella Wickham, Margot's ever-watchful lady's maid, sidled up to her on the terrace. "Well," Stella said, her tone laced with dry amusement, "imagine that—a gathering at Blackwell Manor without quarrels, murders, or mayhem. Progress, wouldn't you say?"

Margot laughed softly, the sound as light as the spring breeze that ruffled her hair. "Is it progress, Stella, or merely a reprieve?"

"I suppose only time will tell," Stella quipped before slipping away into the house, leaving Margot to her thoughts.

The clinking of footsteps on the stone path drew Margot's attention toward the garden, where a lone figure approached. Inspector Simon Grant, hat in hand, ascended the terrace steps with his usual air of calm self-assurance.

"Inspector," Margot greeted him, her eyes glinting with curiosity. "To what do we owe this surprise? Surely you've had your fill of manor life for one season?"

Simon raised an eyebrow, the faintest trace of a smile tugging at his lips. "I wouldn't miss the conclusion to your latest escapade, Lady Blackwell. Though I must say, your villagers are far more cooperative than your suspects."

Margot smirked. "Perhaps that's because they don't keep quite so many skeletons in their closets."

"If you're here to find trouble, Inspector," Stella called from the doorway, her tone cheeky, "you've come to the wrong party."

"I'm only here," Simon replied with a pointed look toward Margot, "to ensure Lady Margot doesn't start it."

Margot chuckled, shaking her head. "I suppose I shall have to behave, then."

Simon held out his arm, an unspoken invitation for Margot to join him. She hesitated for the briefest of moments before taking it, allowing him to lead her down the lantern-lit path that wound through the garden.

———

As the final notes of the evening drifted into the air, Simon and Margot found themselves alone in the centre of the garden, where a string quartet played a soft waltz under the stars. For once, the constant tension that so often defined their conversations seemed to dissipate, replaced by a quiet understanding.

Simon turned to her, his expression unreadable. "You know," he said after a moment, "I never did thank you properly for your... assistance in solving this case."

Margot arched an eyebrow. "Assistance, Inspector? I believe it was you who tagged along on my deductions."

Simon chuckled, inclining his head slightly. "Fair enough. But credit where it's due—you have a knack for unravelling chaos."

"As do you," Margot replied, her voice softer than usual. "Though I must admit, we make a rather effective pair."

Simon paused, his gaze meeting hers, and for a moment, the world around them seemed to fall away. "Perhaps," he said, his tone thoughtful, "this isn't the last time Blackwell Manor finds itself caught in a mystery."

"Perhaps not," Margot agreed, a hint of a smile playing on her lips.

The music swelled quietly in the background as the two shared a subtle but meaningful dance, their movements unhurried yet full of understanding. There was no need for further words; the connection between them had already begun to shift from rivalry to partnership, tinged with the faintest possibility of something more.

———

As the evening drew to a close, Madame Celeste took to the stage, her presence quiet but commanding. The crowd hushed as she began to speak, her voice carrying the elegance of a woman who had once captivated audiences across Europe.

"My friends," she began, her gaze sweeping over the gathered villagers and guests, "tonight has reminded me of something I had forgotten: the beauty of small stages and quiet audiences. It has been an honour to witness such talent, and I am grateful to Lady Margot Blackwell for showing me that there is… grace in simplicity."

Tears glistened in her eyes as she stepped down from the stage, where Margot met her with a gentle embrace. "Thank you, Celeste," Margot said, her voice warm. "I hope this is just the beginning of a new chapter for you."

Celeste nodded, her smile tinged with sadness but also hope. "Perhaps it is. And perhaps, my dear Margot, you are more than the mistress of this manor—you are its heart."

Later, as the lanterns dimmed and the guests began to drift home, Margot retreated to the study, where Simon and Stella were waiting with glasses of port in hand. The three of them raised their glasses in a quiet toast, the weight of the past weeks hanging in the air like an unspoken promise.

"To Blackwell Manor," Margot said simply, "and to the peace that I hope will follow."

"Here's to Blackwell Manor," Stella quipped with a wry smile, "having one uneventful season ahead."

Simon smirked, raising his glass higher. "And here's to ensuring Lady Margot keeps herself out of trouble—though I suspect that's wishful thinking."

Margot chuckled softly as she clinked her glass against theirs, feeling, for the first time in weeks, a sense of calm. The storm had passed, and while the scars of its chaos would take time to heal, the manor, and those who called it home, were ready to move forward.

The case was solved, the household slowly returning to its rhythms, but something had fundamentally changed.

"The world is changing," Simon said quietly, coming to stand beside her. "Not even Blackwell Manor can remain untouched."

Margot nodded. "The war changed everything. We try to cling to the old ways, the familiar patterns, but underneath it all..."

"Underneath it all, we're all just trying to find our place in this new world," Simon finished.

She turned to face him. "Evelyn, Irene, Celeste—they were all fighting their own battles against a society that wouldn't let them be who they needed to be. Celeste, clinging to fame that was slipping away. Irene, desperate for recognition her talent deserved. Evelyn, trying to secure her future in a world that offered women like her few options."

"And yet, here you stand," Simon observed. "Lady Margot Blackwell, mistress of her domain, detective in her own right."

Margot smiled, a genuine expression that softened her features. "Perhaps that's the true mystery solved here—not just who killed Evelyn Linwood, but how each of us chooses to face this brave new world. With grace or desperation, with integrity or deception."

Blackwell Manor, she thought with quiet resolve, would endure. And so would she.

The End

AFTERWORD

Thank you for reading ***Murder of a Fake Diva***. I really hope you enjoyed reading it as much as I had writing it!

If you have a minute, please consider leaving a review on Amazon, GoodReads and/or Bookbub.

Many thanks in advance for your support!

MURDER OF A NOTORIOUS GENTLEMAN

SNEAK PEEK

SNEAK PEEK

*L*ady Margot Blackwell pressed her gloved hand against the window of her gleaming Bentley as the Brighton Pavilion emerged through the morning mist, its fantastical silhouette unmistakable even through the gauzy sea air. The onion domes and minarets rose like an extravagant confection against the pale sky, part Oriental fantasy, part royal folly, an Edwardian remnant that somehow managed to look both absurdly dated and eternally fashionable. She smiled to herself. The Pavilion suited her cousin Rosalind perfectly—both were ostentatious, impossible to ignore, and utterly indifferent to convention.

"I shall never understand," remarked Stella Wickham, adjusting her cloche hat with a perfunctory pat, "why anyone would build such a monstrosity by the sea. Salt ruins everything eventually." Stella, Lady Margot's ever-practical lady's maid, had the unique privilege of speaking with a frankness few others would dare, a habit that Margot found both vexing and oddly reassuring.

Margot raised an eyebrow. "Including your disposition, it seems."

"Travel does that, my lady. Especially when one is squashed beside three hatboxes that insisted on coming along." Stella glanced pointedly at the luggage crowding the Bentley's leather interior.

"The hatboxes were non-negotiable. We're in Brighton now. Appearances matter more than comfort."

"So I've heard," Stella muttered. "Though I suspect your cousin cares precious little for either."

The Bentley purred to a halt before the Pavilion's grand entrance, where a slender figure stood waiting, a paint-splattered smock covering what might have been a fashionable dropped-waist dress. Rosalind Hayworth waved wildly, her blonde bob escaping its pins in artistic disarray.

"Margot! At last!" Rosalind called out, rushing forward before Williams, the chauffeur, could properly assist Lady Margot from the motorcar. "You're late, which I expected, but you look splendid, which I also expected. Is that Chanel? Marvellous!"

"Hello, cousin." Margot embraced Rosalind warmly, despite the risk to her travelling ensemble. "I see you've been painting already this morning."

"Morning, afternoon... time blurs when inspiration strikes." Rosalind made a theatrical gesture toward the Pavilion. "Brighton has been positively dreary without you. Nothing but the usual scandals and whispers, which aren't half as entertaining without your commentary."

Stella emerged from the Bentley with significantly less

ceremony, her practical hands already reaching for the smaller bags. "Shall I arrange for the luggage, my lady?"

"Please do, Stella." Margot turned back to her cousin. "I trust you've prepared rooms for us?"

"Of course! The Nash suite. It has the best light for portrait studies." Rosalind's eyes gleamed with mischief. "I've half a mind to paint you this visit. The Lady Detective of Sussex would make a splendid subject."

Margot winced at the title. "I prefer not to encourage that particular moniker."

"Too late. The Gazette printed it after the Diva affair." Rosalind linked her arm through Margot's and guided her up the Pavilion steps. "Come inside. I have an exhibition to show you that's causing quite the delicious stir. Even the Bright Young Things are scandalised, and you know how difficult that is these days."

The Pavilion's interior was as excessive as its exterior—a riot of colour and ornamentation that assaulted the senses. Dragons coiled across ceilings, palm-leaf columns supported fantastical chandeliers, and everywhere mirrors multiplied the splendour to dizzying effect. Rosalind led them through corridors adorned with Chinese wallpaper and past rooms where royalty had once entertained with reckless abandon.

"Your exhibition is inside the Pavilion?" Margot asked, surprised. "I hadn't realised you'd secured such prestigious patronage."

"Oh, not the official exhibition. That opens next week at Bellingham's gallery. This is my private collection, the portraits too scandalous for public display." Rosalind's voice dropped to a theatrical whisper. "The ones where I've painted people as they truly are, rather than as they wish to be seen. Absolutely modern—no flattery, no soft focus."

They arrived at a large salon where canvases of various sizes had been arranged around the perimeter. Stella, having dispatched the luggage upstairs, joined them at the doorway, her practical gaze sweeping the room with undisguised curiosity.

"Well," said Stella, eyeing a particularly unflattering portrait of a corpulent gentleman, "I see subtlety isn't in fashion this season."

Rosalind laughed. "Brighton has never had much use for subtlety, Stella. Here, everyone is exactly who they pretend not to be, especially since the war ended. All that desperate gaiety covering the cracks."

Margot moved slowly around the room, studying each portrait. Rosalind had always possessed a remarkable talent, but these new works showed a maturity and confidence that surpassed her earlier efforts. The paintings were bold, almost Vorticist in style, each subject rendered with technical precision and an almost uncomfortable honesty—every line of dissipation, every shadow of discontent captured with merciless clarity.

"You've improved," Margot said, genuinely impressed. "These are extraordinary, Rosalind."

"Extraordinary enough to cause several cancelled dinner invitations," Rosalind replied cheerfully. "Lady Harrington nearly fainted when she saw her husband's portrait. Said I'd made him look like a walrus with indigestion."

"And had you?" Stella asked.

"Only because he does." Rosalind gestured toward a covered canvas in the corner. "But that's nothing compared to my masterpiece. The portrait that's made me simultaneously the most sought-after and most reviled artist in Brighton."

With a flourish, she pulled away the cloth to reveal a large portrait of a man in his forties. He was handsome in a conventional way—dark hair, fashionable clothes, an air of self-satisfaction—but Rosalind had painted him with a shadow across his features that suggested something unpleasant lurking beneath the polished exterior. His smile, though perfect, seemed to conceal a sneer, and his eyes held a calculating coldness that made Margot instinctively wary.

"Reginald Myers," Rosalind announced. "Brighton's most notorious gentleman."

Margot studied the portrait, noting the technical brilliance; the perfect rendering of the silk waistcoat, the exquisite detailing of the platinum watch chain, but also the subtle indictment in every brushstroke. "I take it Mr Myers was not pleased with the result?"

"On the contrary. He adored it. Said I was the only person who'd ever seen him clearly." Rosalind tapped her chin thoughtfully. "Which was, I suppose, not entirely a compliment, given what I saw."

"And what was that?" Margot asked.

"A man who collects secrets like others collect art. Myers knows everything about everyone in Brighton. He cultivates gossip the way some men cultivate roses—with careful attention and occasional ruthless pruning."

Stella snorted. "Sounds delightful."

"He's coming to dinner tonight," Rosalind added. "Along with several others who've sat for me. You'll see for yourself."

Before Margot could respond, a discreet knock interrupted them. A servant appeared at the doorway, announcing that tea had been prepared in the Music Room and that Mrs Phelps had arrived early.

"Audrey is here?" Margot's face brightened. "I didn't know she was in Brighton."

"She's practically a fixture now," Rosalind explained as they made their way through the Pavilion's labyrinthine corridors. "Runs half the charitable initiatives in town. The Brighton Ladies' Benevolent Society, the Fishermen's Relief Fund, the Hospital Committee—Audrey has her perfectly manicured fingers in every philanthropic pie."

The Music Room, with its crimson and gold decorations and enormous crystal chandelier, provided a dramatic setting for afternoon tea. Audrey Phelps stood by the windows, her elegant figure silhouetted against the light. At the sight of Margot, she rushed forward, arms outstretched.

"Margot! How wonderful to see you." Her embrace was warm but brief, her movements retaining the controlled grace Margot remembered from childhood. Her bobbed hair gleamed like polished mahogany, and her dress, though modest by current standards, was unmistakably from Paris.

"Too long," Margot agreed, studying her old friend. Audrey looked well, perhaps a touch thinner than Margot recalled, with faint shadows beneath her eyes that suggested recent strain, but otherwise as composed and elegant as ever.

They settled around a table laden with delicate sandwiches, scones, and pastries. Stella positioned herself discreetly nearby, close enough to attend to Margot's needs but far enough to allow private conversation.

"Rose Congou?" Margot asked hopefully as Audrey poured the tea.

"Darjeeling, I'm afraid," Audrey replied with a sympathetic smile. "Still searching for your perfect blend?"

"Endlessly. I've tried every tea shop in Kent without success." Margot sighed dramatically. "Brighton was my last hope."

"The lengths to which the aristocracy will go for a particular leaf steeped in hot water," Rosalind teased, lighting a cigarette in a long ivory holder. "Meanwhile, the rest of us make do with whatever doesn't taste of dishwater."

Audrey laughed, but the sound held a nervous edge. "Your cousin exaggerates, as always. Though I must say, Margot, your dedication to this quest borders on obsession."

"Not obsession. Discernment." Margot accepted the teacup with a nod of thanks. "One must have standards, even in Brighton."

"Especially in Brighton," Audrey corrected. "This town thrives on appearances. The right tea, the right dress, the right connections... they're currency here."

"Speaking of connections," Rosalind interjected, blowing a perfect smoke ring toward the ceiling, "I was just showing Margot my portrait of Reginald Myers. You've met him, haven't you, Audrey?"

The change in Audrey was subtle but unmistakable. Her fingers tightened around her teacup, and a flicker of something—anxiety? fear?—crossed her face before her composure reasserted itself.

"Yes, of course. Mr Myers is quite involved in local society." Her voice remained steady, but Margot noticed she had begun to straighten her gloves, smoothing invisible wrinkles with deliberate care. "His contributions to the Hospital Fund have been most generous."

"How interesting," Margot remarked, watching her friend closely. "Rosalind paints him as rather more complex than a simple philanthropist."

"Rosalind sees what others miss," Audrey replied carefully. "It's what makes her art so... uncomfortable."

"Uncomfortable but truthful," Rosalind declared, helping herself to a scone. "Myers himself said so."

"Did he?" Audrey's voice had grown quieter. "Well, Mr Myers has always appreciated honesty. In others, if not in himself."

The conversation drifted to safer topics—the upcoming Brighton Season, mutual acquaintances, the latest London fashions—but Margot continued to observe Audrey with quiet attention. Something about Myers had disturbed her normally unflappable friend, and Margot found herself curious about the nature of their acquaintance.

As they finished their tea, Audrey glanced at the ornate clock and rose with evident relief. "I'm afraid I must go. The Benevolent Society meets at four, and I have reports to review beforehand."

"Will you join us for dinner?" Rosalind asked. "Myers will be here, along with Bellingham and the Finchley party."

Again, that momentary stiffness. "I'm afraid not. Prior engagement. But perhaps tomorrow?" Audrey kissed Margot's cheek. "We have so much to catch up on."

After Audrey had departed, Margot turned to Rosalind. "She seemed rather tense at the mention of Mr Myers."

"Everyone in Brighton tenses at the mention of Myers," Rosalind replied with a shrug. "He has that effect on people. Like a sudden draft in a warm room."

Margot sipped the last of her tea, finding it pleasant but unremarkable. Not Rose Congou but perhaps a suitable substitute until her quest bore fruit.

"Well," she said finally, "I look forward to meeting this notorious gentleman for myself."

From her position by the door, Stella caught Margot's eye. "Notorious gentlemen rarely live up to their reputations, my lady. Though they do have a habit of exceeding them in all the wrong ways."

Margot smiled. As always, Stella had cut directly to the heart of the matter. Brighton, with its façades and fantasies, its Pavilion and pretensions, was the perfect setting for illusions. And Reginald Myers, it seemed, was master of them all.

"Come," she said, rising from the table. "I should rest before dinner. Something tells me this evening will require all my attention."

———

You can order your copy of **Murder of a Notorious Gentleman** at any good online retailer.

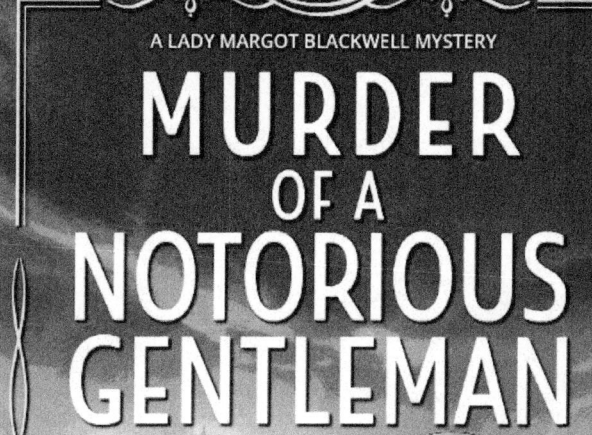

A LADY MARGOT BLACKWELL MYSTERY

MURDER
OF A
NOTORIOUS
GENTLEMAN

AMBER CREWES

ALSO BY AMBER CREWES

Xylose Treats and Killer Sweets

Yummy Pies and Someone Dies

Zucchini Chips and Poisoned Lips

THE SPRING HARBOR COZY MYSTERY SERIES

Hair Today, Dead Tomorrow

A Short Cut to Murder

Snip Once, Die Twice

Killing Off Loose Ends

Curl Up and Die

Bangs, Bullies and Betrayal

Permed to Deadly Perfection

A Hairy Scary Christmas

A Grim Trim in a Gym

The Blonde that didn't Respond

Mousse, Murder and Mayem

Dye Hard with a Vengeance

THE LADY MARGOT BLACKWELL MYSTERY SERIES

Murder of a Fake Diva

Murder of a Notorious Gentleman

Murder of a Greedy Accountant

NEWSLETTER SIGNUP

Want **FREE** COPIES OF FUTURE **AMBER CREWES**
BOOKS, FIRST NOTIFICATION OF NEW RELEASES,
CONTESTS AND GIVEAWAYS?

GO TO THE LINK BELOW TO SIGN UP TO THE
NEWSLETTER AND GET A **FREE PREQUEL STORY**!

www.AmberCrewes.com/cozylist

Printed in Dunstable, United Kingdom